Soul Redemption

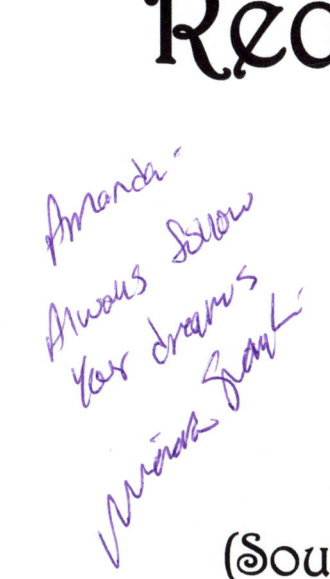

(Soul series book 2)

Soul Redemption

By Miranda Shanklin

This novel is a work of fiction. Any resemblance to actual persons, living or deceased is coincidental. The characters, names, plots, or incidents within are the product of the author's imagination. References to actual events or locations are included to give the fiction a sense of reality.

Copyright 2016, Miranda Shanklin

All rights reserved. No part of this may be reproduced, stored, or transmitted in any form, by any means without written consent from Miranda Shanklin.

Cover design, Paper & Sage Designs 2014.

ISBN: (Trade Paperback): 978-1539835523

(E-book)

DEDICATION

To my husband and children who are just as excited about this adventure as I am. I would not be able to do it without your love and support.

Other books by Miranda Shanklin

Soul Journey
Soul Series Book 1

Soul Knowledge
Soul Series Book 3

Soul Freedom
Soul Series Book 4

Soul Discovery
Soul Series Book 5

Coming soon:

Guardians of the Origin trilogy

Miranda Shanklin

ACKNOWLEDGMENTS

I have so many people that have helped me get to where I am today. My parents have always instilled in me the belief that I can do anything I put my mind to. They have always supported me in everything that I have tried and encouraged me and even given me a hard push when it was needed. I can't ever express how much their love and support has helped to shape me into the person that I am and given me the confidence to chase my dreams.

My husband and children have sacrificed so that I can chase this dream. I am unbelievably blessed that they have picked up the slack and taken care of the house and our animals while I have been lost in my own world writing. They have supported me and encouraged me as I embarked on this new journey.

My friend Ari, who has spent hours on end reviewing, correcting, and giving advice. I could not have gotten through this book without her.

My friend Amanda who was there in the early stages when this was just an idea I was throwing around was a tremendous help. She let me bounce ideas off her and gave some advice on some different ways to see it. I may not have kept the idea the way we talked about it but bouncing my ideas off her was the best start I could get.

I also received amazing support and information from fellow authors Ednah Walters and Suzan Tisdale. They have opened up their e-mails to me and helped to guide me through the process of publishing. I wouldn't have even known where to start without these wonderful ladies. They are amazing authors and I am glad that after I read their work and fell in love with their stories that I reached out to them and asked for help. I was rewarded so much more than I ever thought.

CHAPTER 1

It was a quiet but stressful winter. Months have gone by since we fought, and won, against the Council's top assassin. While we've been preparing for their next attack, other witches have messaged or emailed us, which would be great if they were supportive, but since they have been threatening, or hateful, it has made for a very stressful situation. With the cold winter weather we had an excuse to not leave the house much except for school. Now that spring is here, and it is getting warmer, we will have to venture out into our small town.

At the end of our battle with the Peter, he warned us that he was just the first attempt. The Council would be sending others. The problem is, we have no idea who, what, where, or when it will occur. We have been on edge watching for any sign of an attack, but there hasn't been anything. I am starting to think they are just going to leave us alone, now that they know what they are up against. Unfortunately, our parents don't agree.

"Mom, if they were going to attack again with some other tactic, they would have by now. They wouldn't have given us all this time to learn to better control our magick and improve with more experience. They would have sent someone right away, when we were still weak from the fight with Peter," I argue exchanging a pleading glance with Chase for help. It is the same conversation we have been having with our parents for the last couple of months. Of course, she responds the way that she always does.

"They are trying to lure you into a false sense of security. They want you to believe they are not going to continue trying to destroy you, so you will let your guard down."

Everybody in the room groans as the same argument starts once again. Landon has finally had enough of the whole thing and tries to put an end to it. "Look, we don't know what the Council has planned. The only thing we know for sure, is the rest of our world is upset with us, and we need to focus on that for now. I think we need to put this argument to the side and focus on the problems that are on our heads at the moment."

Chase is relieved. His body visibly relaxes when he didn't have to come between me and my mom again on this matter. He agrees with Landon. "Now that it has warmed up and we will be out more, we really have to watch for other witches. I still don't understand why they are so upset with us. Were we supposed to stay in that endless cycle of misery just so the Council would be happy and nothing ever changed?"

Penelope sighs. "It's not that we should have stayed in that situation. They are scared. Nobody knows how the Council is going to react to us breaking free and then stopping our assassination." She clasps her hands in front of her as if pleading for us to understand. "You have to remember, we came out of a fight with the one person the Council has always used to get rid of their problems, and not one of us was hurt. That much power in one group of witches scares them. They don't know what kind of people we are. All they have seen is our self-destructive behavior as Annisa never made a choice and created a love triangle that ended badly for all of us in life after life. To them we are a group of immature teenagers with way too much power." She drops her head to her hands when she is done.

As the guilt of the whole mess weighs on me I sit back in my seat and think about what she is saying. In the beginning, I was unable to determine if Landon or Chase was my soul mate and I had a relationship with both of them at the same time. Apparently, it was worse that in every life cycle before this one, I was slutty too because I always had a physical relationship with both of them as well. Penelope tried to help in the beginning and cast a spell to reveal my true soul mate. The problem with that was, it was what the Council was waiting for in order to punish us.

Penelope was only trying to help, she had the most lenient punishment and was born in each life with her powers and magick at birth instead of waiting to get either when she turned 16 like the rest of us. Chase and Landon only used their magick against each other in retaliation and anger, their punishment wasn't as harsh as mine either. As they hurt innocent people in the crossfire of their war, they did have a stronger punishment than Penelope. They received a portion of their power at age 16, but not their memories until after my punishment took effect. My offense was the worst of them all. I was the one that carried on with both Chase and Landon. I was the one that refused to make a decision and listen to my heart, so my punishment was the most severe. I would only receive a portion of my power when I turned 16, but none of my memories until I made a choice.

In order for us to break free from this cycle, I had to make a decision, and the four of us had to act like mature adults instead of spoiled children. I had to choose on which one I wanted to be with before having a physical relationship with either of them, except I didn't have my memories of previous lives, and nobody was allowed to share information with me until after I made my decision. In every life before this one, I repeated the same mistakes. This time around, we finally handled the situation correctly, and broke free from the endless cycle of pain and heartache.

Chase looks over with sympathetic eyes, reaches for my hand, and tries to comfort me. "Baby, you heard Rayne. She said the Council planted the idea that she was my soul mate and that Landon was yours. They set us up from the beginning. As soon as they realized they wouldn't be able to control us they started their plan to destroy us. It wasn't your fault, they manipulated everyone involved to get the result they wanted."

I sigh as my shoulders slump in defeat. "I know. I just wish I had been mature enough before now to handle the whole thing. I'm really ashamed of the way I've behaved in my past lives. I know it's not all my fault, but really, I'm the only one to blame for sleeping with both you and Landon before I made my decision." A jealous expression passes across his face so fast that if I hadn't been watching, I might have missed it. We have come to terms with our pasts. The jealousy is gone almost as quickly as it arrived. He leans over, gives me a sweet kiss, turns to look at Penelope with his brows raised.

Glancing back and forth between them, my confusion must show on my face. Penelope gives Chase a glare before she turns to me with a look of defeat. "There is not a spell that would make anyone have sex with anyone else. The spell would dissipate before that. This is something that has been natural to magick since the beginning. Magick is pure. It is the wieldier who decides to use it as Dark, Light, or both. Since it is pure, there is no way to use it to force someone into intimacy." She states.

Penelope continues quietly. "There are however, spells that can make you drop your inhibitions to the point where you don't care that what you are doing is not something you would normally do. It's the way people who use Dark magick have found to go around the law of magick that doesn't let you use it force someone to sleep with you. I don't have any proof, but I think that spell has been used on you in most of your lifetimes. Somehow this time, you were able to avoid it. The only thing I can think of, is that whoever was casting the spell, didn't know where you were this time. We weren't all in the same place for our entire lifetime. The Council couldn't tell whoever it was where you were, without everyone finding out that they were behind the whole situation from the beginning." She summarizes.

My jaw drops as I realize what she is saying, and the full effect of what happened sinks in. My hands fly to my hips as I snarl "You are just now telling me about this?"

She glares at Chase again, who's waiting for her to continue. "I didn't have any proof. It is just a theory I've been thinking about since our last lifetime. Like I said, we've always been together since we were babies, so I've always known you better than anyone else. Each lifetime I was astonished when you started sleeping with both Landon and Chase. It has never been consistent with your personality." She stands up and starts pacing. Her hands wrap around her abdomen and she avoids eye contact with anyone. "So, at the end of the last life cycle I told our parents about my theory. That is why they kept us separated until it was time to make your choice." She offers.

I turn to Chase. He is staring at his hands in his lap. I can feel my face turning read with anger. I can't sit as I try to control my magick from lashing out at him. I clench my hands into fists to try and stop them from shaking. As I am pacing around the room he continues to stare at his hands. My voice is surprisingly even as I finally speak. "I can see that you have known about this for a while. Why didn't you tell me sooner?" I ask.

When he looks up, he gasps as he is faced with my anger. Instead of him pleading with me as I expect, he meets my anger with his own. "It was Penelope's theory, and I wasn't sure how to tell my girlfriend that I thought I knew why she kept sleeping with my best friend." He shouts.

I stop pacing and stare at him while I attempt to control my emotions. I take a deep breath and try to look at the situation logically. As I process this new information and come to terms with it, I start to laugh. Everyone else looks at me like I have gone crazy. When I finally calm down enough to explain I begin, "All this time I was thinking I had to be this really self-centered person to put us through this so many times, and it turns out that I'm just a hormonal teenager."

My dad looks at me with a raised brow. "Well, when you put it that way it does sound like a soap opera." With that nobody can hold their laughter in. Now that we have been able to find some humor in the situation we are able to get back on topic and not be so sensitive about what anyone is saying. Chase and Penelope's mom is the first to try bringing the conversation back to where it needs to be. "I understand that everyone is scared about what the Council is going to do, but I don't understand why the other witches think all of this is your fault. It doesn't make any sense to me why you four are being targeted. You were a victims in this whole thing."

Landon has been quiet but finally voices his theory. "I think the Council has taken some notes from high school. I think they may have sent a few people out to start some rumors about how we broke free, and how the Council is in hiding because of what we are trying to do."

We all look at him stunned. My dad is the first to recover, "That makes a lot of sense. They are trying to get the other witches to come after you so it looks like they are still trying to keep the peace, instead of trying to kill you for no reason. It would also explain why they haven't sent anyone else after you. They could play it off that Peter was crazy, that he truly believed that Chase was supposed to be with his daughter, and that he was working on his own and not under their order. So now, if they just sit back and let the others believe the rumors they had started, they won't have to get their hands dirty."

We realize that he is most likely right, and we each become lost in our own thoughts about how to proceed from here. This is a good plan on their end. It could easily bring about their desired actions without making them look bad.

Chase is the first one to react. He looks around at everyone in the room and I can see the anger in his eyes before he begins. "So, they punish us for acting like teenagers, when that is exactly what we are. Then, they act like spoiled kids that want to hurt others, with no truth to what they are saying or doing?"

Landon's mom answers this time. "You have to remember, the only thing anyone else knows is what they have seen. They've seen the four of you behaving like spoiled children throwing a fit whenever you didn't get what you wanted for many lifetimes. They have no idea that your actions were justified, nor that you were under any spells. They don't want to take the chance that the Council is truly trying to protect them and they act out against them. Due to your actions, they are reacting the way they feel is right."

Chase's anger deflates as fast as it surged forward. "I see what you mean. I don't understand why nobody else sees what the Council is doing."

My dad sighs. "For the most part, most witches are left alone to live out their life cycles in peace. There is no reason for them to think anything bad about the Council. The only ones that have anything to fear are the most powerful, such as you four. As long as they are not powerful enough to pose a threat to the Council, and they do not question the system or those that run it, there is no reason for the Council to even think twice about them. Most witches live in this state of ignorance, simply because they have no reason to question it."

Penelope voices what we are all thinking and trying to find a way to say, "Since they don't know any better, and they have never actually met us, they are just going to assume that we are the bad guys, and they are going to rally behind the Council to protect them and their way of life?"

I look up at her defeated. "Yep, that's the way I understand it too. Looks like we're going to have to try and find a way to convince the people that are going to try and destroy us, that we are not trying to destroy them. Should be interesting."

CHAPTER 2

The next day at school everything is normal. Everyone has gotten used to Landon and me not being together anymore, but still really good friends. I chuckle when I think about the rumors that were flying around the school when Chase and Penelope first moved here. It was quite the drama for Landon and I to split and start dating Chase and Penelope. All they saw was a couple that had been together for as long as they could remember, now broken up and dating the new students but still really close. We couldn't tell them that we were connected and share an unbreakable bond.

With everything that we have had going on, Landon and I have pulled away from our other friends. We aren't really in the center of the group anymore, so sometimes it takes a while before we hear the rumors that are buzzing around. When I finally notice something is going on, I stop one of the girls on my cheerleading squad and ask her what it is.

"You haven't heard? There are two new students. A really cute boy and a really pretty girl started here this morning. We haven't had new students here in forever, and then this year we have had five. If our little town keeps growing like this, we might actually get a mall or something!" My stomach is suddenly in knots. Every time we get a new student in our school my life turns into chaos.

During lunch I can tell Penelope, Chase, and Landon are no more excited about the news than I am. They look like their stomachs are in upside down. Because we're connected and have merged our magick, we can feel the emotions of the others constantly. I'm usually able to push their emotions to the back of my mind, but since we are anxious about what is going on, I can feel them as much as my own anxiety. The fact that we can talk into each other's minds helps us to keep our secrets. We don't use it very often because we don't want anyone to find out that we have this skill. We can either talk to the group all together, or just with one other person. It is really helpful in fighting situations, but it can become habit forming.

I feel the connection open and I shake my head. I don't want whoever the new students are to become suspicious of us not talking about it. Penelope gives me a weird look as I shake my head, so she must be the one who opened it. Instantly I feel her close it rather than ask why.

I sit down at the table as I address our small group. "I can tell I'm not the only one who feels like more new students are not a good thing. Has anyone seen either of them yet?" They shake their heads no. I'm trying to figure out how in a school this small none of us have any classes with either of them. It's odd, but not unheard of. There are plenty of people in my grade I don't share classes with, so I don't think this is something that we really need to worry about.

Chase is still concerned though. "I understand that it's normal to not have either of them in my classes." He looks around to make sure that nobody is listening in before he continues. "What are the odds that they wouldn't have any classes all four of us?"

Landon seems just as concerned as Chase but shrugs it off. "The day is only half over. Maybe they'll have a class with one of us this afternoon."

Penelope reaches into her bag and pulls out a hand mirror to check her makeup. "The only thing that I've found out is that one of them is in my grade and one of them is in yours. I think the girl is in mine and the boy is in yours. I am not positive yet, that's just what I've been able to put together from the rumors flying around." She grins and makes sure she has our undivided attention before moving on. "You should hear some of them. If I believed them all, I would think we had a shape shifter here or something. Some are drooling over how cute they both are, and some are acting like they wouldn't give them the time of day." She laughs as she finishes filling us in on the more ridiculous rumors she has heard that morning.

I voice my thoughts. "We don't know if this has anything to do with us. They could have moved here for a number of other reasons. We are assuming a lot by automatically thinking it's about us." I offer rationally. They look at me as if I had grown a second head.

Landon is the first to recover. "When was the last time that someone moved to this town that didn't have anything to do with us?" He stares me down.

I think about it for a minute. "In sixth grade." I smile triumphantly at him and Chase and Penelope laugh at us.

By the end of lunch we have managed to reduce our anxieties to a more reasonable level. We decide there's nothing we can do about the new students being here, and we will just have to deal with whatever comes our way. As soon as I walk into my next class I know Penelope is right about the new boy being in my grade. The rumors about him being cute are true. I am instantly given dirty looks as soon as I walk into the room. One girl even goes so far as to say under her breath as I walk by, "Are you going to try and get to this one before any of us have a chance too?"

I ignore her and walk to my seat, start getting my book out of my bag, and get ready for class to begin, pretending like I don't see the dirty looks or hear the snide comments. I understand why they think that. From what they could see when Chase and Penelope moved here, it looked like I dropped Landon as soon as someone new was available. Since I can't tell them the real story, I have to let them believe what they want and ignore it. They will see soon enough, I have no intentions of ever being apart from Chase. He is my soul mate, the one person who was created to complete me, and I will never want anyone else.

When class gets started, I can't look behind me to see the new boy without making it obvious what I am doing, so I have to sit there with him a few seats behind me. I never understood when people said they could feel someone boring holes in the back of their head with their eyes, until today. Of course, it is possible that I'm overreacting because I haven't actually seen him yet. I can sense him, but it isn't the same as with Penelope, Chase and Landon. We have not had normal interactions with other witches, so I'm not sure if this is a normal reaction.

By the time class is over, I am so edgy that I jump up when the bell rings and bolt from the classroom. Chase is outside the door so we can walk to our next class together. He could sense how stressed I was getting during class. I look around to make sure that nobody is paying any attention to us. "Penelope is right. The new boy is in our grade. He was in my last class. I didn't get a chance to look at him since the girls are being petty about another new boy coming to the school. I'm sure that will die down in the next day when they realize that I will never leave your side, though. Anyway, he was sitting behind me. It felt like he was staring holes in the back of my head the entire hour."

As I finish saying this, a boy I have never seen before walks past us. He doesn't look in our direction. Chase watches him as he walks the same way that we need to go, with a thoughtful look on his face. "Maybe you overreacted. I can sense him, but it is different. I can't tell if he is a witch or what. When he walked by us, he didn't even look our way. If he was here to mess with us, he would have at least tried to look at us and see what we were doing. I don't think we have enough information to figure anything out yet."

I agree with him. We have to hurry to our next class to keep from being late. We walk through the door hand in hand, and find the new boy surrounded by a group of girls vying for his attention. I raise my eyebrow at the interest he is getting and then start laughing as I figure out what is going on. Chase gives me a look that lets me know he has no idea what is happening or why I am laughing. I clue him in on how teenage girls can think. "They want to make sure that he sees them first. As long as they create a wall around him, he won't be able to see me, so they think that will give them a better chance. After what happened when you moved here, they think that I'm going to try and grab him up too."

I turn so we can go to our seats and stop dead in my tracks. There's a girl leaning on Chase's desk. Her shirt is unbuttoned a little too far. She doesn't seem to notice me standing right next to Chase holding his hand. She looks at him with sultry eyes. "Now that there is someone new for Annisa to pounce on, you will soon be free to see what a real woman can do for you."

I am so furious that I am fighting my magick to keep it inside of me. Chase gives my hand a squeeze and looks at her like he is bored. "I know you're a senior, and think you are the best thing around, but I really don't think the desperate thing is attractive. Just because you have run through the boys in this town and not been able to keep any of them happy doesn't mean that I will jump into bed with you. And just so you know, Annisa and I are fine. We have no intention of splitting up. Ever."

As he is saying this, her face turns darker shades of red. She looks around and sees everyone in the class is watching us. Then, she sees me grinning. I'm trying really hard to not laugh at her expression. She can't think of a quick response to prevent even more damage to her reputation, so she just glares at us both and leaves the room. As soon as she's gone, the girls start whispering and texting about what happened.

By the time this class is over the entire school will know what happened. When I realize how bad this is going to get for her, I no longer feel like laughing.

I feel really bad for her and what she will be dealing with, but a small part of me feels like she got what she deserves for trying to swoop in and steal Chase away. As I sit down in my seat, I see the new boy is watching us with a great deal of interest. As soon as he sees me I notice him watching us, he turns around and faces the front of the room. Chase is still watching me to see how I am going to react to the other situation, so he doesn't notice we are being watched.

I can feel Chase watching me closely to make sure that I am alright after our confrontation. I look at him, "I'm fine. I knew it was going to happen. I just thought it would be in your other classes when I wasn't there."

By the look on his face I can tell that's exactly what has been happening all day in his other classes. I groan in frustration. He starts to say something, but the teacher begins his lecture so our conversation is cut short. He tries to open the connection between us so he can still talk to me, but I keep the connection closed. I am not ready to talk about it yet.

He keeps giving me worried glances throughout the class. I stubbornly refuse to let him in to talk to me about it. By the end of class we are both frustrated because neither of us is willing to give in. When the bell rings he looks over and is about to say something, but I start talking before he has a chance to. "I know you want to talk about this, but I'm not ready to yet. Give me some time to process. We can talk about it tonight. I am not shutting you out like I did before. I just need time to process all of this in my head before I can talk about it."

He doesn't look happy. His jaw trembles from clenching his teeth but he agrees. Thankfully, I don't have any more classes with the new boy the rest of the day, so I have plenty of time to process all that has happened. I'm feeling a lot better about the whole situation until Chase stops me on my way to cheerleading practice. Since he usually just watches practice from the shadows so he doesn't distract me, I am surprised when I see him waiting outside of the locker room.

"What's the special occasion that I get to see you before and after practice?" I ask him with a smile as I reach up and give him a kiss. He pulls me closer and deepens the kiss. When he finally lets me up for air, I look at him with a confused look on my face, "What was that about?"

"I have had a very stressful day of girls throwing themselves at me, and I couldn't wait to do that. Then it occurred to me that if these girls were trying to get my attention, then maybe the boys were trying to get yours. I was so jealous. It took everything I had not to barge into your classes and kiss you right in front of everyone." He wraps his arms around my waist and pulls me close.

I laugh. "See, it's not as easy as it sounds to just ignore it. I understand the jealousy. I have been dealing with it all day. Just to let you know, I have not had one boy come up to me and try to get my attention. Well, I have talked to a few boys that are friends of mine, but it was just normal conversation. They even asked how you liked living here."

I don't think he could have stopped the grin that spread across his face. "The reason that I was waiting out here was to let you know that I will be standing on the sidelines watching your practice today. I had the new boy in another one of my classes, and I can't figure him out. I want to keep a closer eye on you since you get lost in the routine and don't always see what is going on off the field. I didn't want you to think something was wrong when you saw me out there. I couldn't help the kiss first though."

"He really is hard to figure out, isn't he?" I agree. "I got the same feeling. It's weird. I think it is a good idea for us to keep our guard up for a while until we figure out what they are doing here, and what they want."

I start to think that we have overreacted again when there is no sign of either of the new kids during practice. We head home and fill our parents in on what happened during the day. The adults are a little nervous about the new kids, but since they haven't done anything, all we can do is wait and see what happens. Penelope has a couple of classes with the new girl, but it seems like she is more interested in the attention she is getting from the boys and didn't appear to have noticed Penelope. We decide that we'll keep an eye out and see what happens.

CHAPTER 3

It happens slowly at first, and it takes me a few days to figure out what is going on. A few of my friends won't look at me anymore, and they refuse to talk to me. I have no idea what happened to make them treat me like this. I have known these people my whole life. It doesn't make sense to me that they are withdrawing completely. Landon admits he is noticing the same thing. Penelope and Chase have moved so many times growing up, they don't seem to notice. They don't know anyone around here well enough for it to really change for them.

Landon and I watch dumbstruck as the people we've grown up with turn their backs on us. The more the new kids show they have no interest in us, the more others to act the same. I am getting suspicious of the new kids and what they are doing to the rest of the school. I have no proof, and no idea what exactly they are doing, so I can't do anything but watch everything unfold.

After about a week, Chase notices we aren't stopped as much in the hall by people that want to talk to me. The girls on the cheerleading squad are no longer trying to give me their ideas for a new routine, but are just going through it without engaging either me or Penelope. After practice he has a strange look on his face and I think he is starting to piece it together too.

That night we meet with our parents in our safe haven, the secure room in my basement. This is the only place that we can go and know for sure that the Council is not listening in on us. There are a number of protection spells on it. The most important are that voices don't travel beyond the room and only those of us that have contributed to the spell are able to open the door.

Since Chase has noticed what is going on, I feel safe bringing it up to the others. "I haven't said anything because I couldn't prove what I was suspecting, and I wasn't sure if I was overreacting. Today, I noticed Chase was starting to see it too. I don't know how they are doing it, but the new kids are alienating us from everyone at school. Somehow the people Landon and I have known our whole lives won't talk to us, or even look at us unless it is completely necessary. They avoid us as much as they can. Even the cheerleading squad doesn't talk to me." I lean back in my chair and let my head fall back as I let out a frustrated breath.

Landon has been nodding the whole time I am talking letting me know that he has noticed this too. "The football team will still follow my instructions and play the strategies that I tell them to, but that's it. They won't talk to me, they won't make suggestions, and off the field, they won't talk to me unless they have to."

Landon's and my mom exchange a worried look. My mom carefully says, "There really is no way for us to know at this point if this is just from them starting rumors you just haven't heard yet, if there is a spell they cast, or if it is simply a phase the kids at school are going through. You have to remember, not everything that happens in the world has to do with magick. Sometimes it is just jealous teenagers. It's probably the other kids trying to make sure you don't try and make a move on the new kids. With the way the situation evolved when Chase and Penelope first moved here, and they don't know the real story, nobody understands what happened. I think you are just overreacting to normal teenage behavior."

Chase voices the concerns that I am feeling. "If you think that, then why did you both look worried before you started that little speech?"

My mom scowls and gives him a stern look to emphasize her disapproval at his tone before she answers him. "The worried look, was because we are afraid that you are so focused on the Council and what they are doing, that you are going to see something sinister in every action that anyone takes. We don't want you to become so paranoid that you accidentally harm an Innocent. You have to remember, most of the town is not from our world and have no idea magick exists. High school is never easy, nobody ever said it was fair, or that teenagers were always rational."

I let out a frustrated sigh. "It's different than the normal teenage drama. We had to deal with that when Chase and Penelope first got here. This is not the same."

Landon's mom gives me a sympathetic look. "Honey, I know you are used to being liked by everyone and you have never had to deal with the other side of the table when it comes to popularity, but you have to understand sometimes these things happen with no involvement from magick."

As we keep talking in circles about this subject, because neither side is willing to concede, Penelope changes the subject. "Okay, we're just going to have to agree to disagree on this for now. I am more concerned with how it feels when we are around them. I can sense them and their magick, but it's not the same as with other witches."

I have to agree that it is something I have been stumped on as well. "Not only that, I have gotten quite a few of my memories now. I know they are coming slowly, but I don't have any flashes of them at all in any of the past life memories that have been revealed to me. I think I have gotten flashes and scenes from each of my lives, and they are not in any of them. How is it possible we have never run into them in any other life?"

Landon's dad answers this time. "It's actually common not to have met every witch, we are spread out throughout the world. You can't expect to have encountered every one at some point. The best way for us to help is if we are present all over. If we were located in close proximity, it would only serve the people in that area, and the rest of the world would suffer for it. As for when you sense them, and their magick, and it feels different, there are a couple reasons that could happen. They may have placed a spell to either shield their magick from you so you wouldn't be able to sense it, or to make it feel different, or they could be regular people that are practicing in magick. There are many different ways normal people have found that allow them to use the earth and her elements and magick, but are not actually witches such as us. They are to be respected, and have the same values as us, but come from a different origin."

We get lost in our thoughts for a few minutes before Chase responds. "So, how are we supposed to know which one they are? I can understand them trying to shield their magick from us so we couldn't sense it, but that didn't happen. So, did their spell not work, or is our magick is too strong to be fooled, or did they just try to change the feel of it? Of course, we will need to discuss the other people and how that is possible, but I don't think that is the case here. I can sense that they are like us, just their magick feels different."

His mom looks relieved "If you can sense they are like us, then that is what we need to focus on. Yes, we need to discuss the other groups of people, but that can wait until the current situation is resolved. Hopefully, we will have time to get into a lot more detail about them before you have to interact with any of them."

My curiosity about the other groups is driving me crazy but they are right, we have to focus on the problem in front of us now. We will have to learn about the potential for a problem with the other groups later. "The most important question we need answered is, if they are like us, why are they trying to shield themselves from us?" None of us have an answer to that question right now. We simply need more information before we can come to a definite conclusion.

I voice another thing that is bothering me about the new kids. "If they are like us, then why do they act like they have absolutely no interest in us? I thought we were like a celebrity group or something, that everyone is always watching us to see what we will do next. It doesn't make sense that if our world is so anxious about what we are planning, and wants to know what we are doing, that they would come this far and just lose interest."

Landon seems to get into his comfort zone now that we are talking about possible strategy. "It actually makes perfect sense. Our world right now is under the belief that we are power hungry and want to take over the Council. If they send in a couple of kids our age to take away our power at the school, they think it will be enough to distract us so they can get into position without us noticing. I don't think they realize we can sense their magick. I also don't think we should let on that we can. The more they think they have the upper hand, the better it is for us. They will gain confidence as they build up to whatever it is they are planning, I think we should let things play out for now and see where they take it."

Penelope looks a little uncomfortable about halfway through what Landon is saying. "I see where that could be a good plan, but I also see where it could backfire drastically. If their plan is to keep us distracted, then the most likely action would be to bring in more witches while we are distracted. That causes a problem in a couple of different ways. It would be hard to keep magick hidden if the town was suddenly overrun by witches. At least one of them would possibly figure out that the land by the beach is 'The Land' they have all been looking for, and that would be really bad."

I can see what she means. "The Council has everyone

believing we are the bad guys and they are trying to get them to do their dirty work for them while they sit up in the Clouds and look like the saviors. The problem we are going to have is not hurting anyone while trying to protect ourselves. If we let them bring in a bunch of witches, the chances of either us or one of them getting hurt increases."

Chase has been quiet until now. "I think the biggest problem we are going to have, is knowing if they are bringing in witches. While we will be able to sense any that come to the school, we won't know how many are actually in the town. We can't be everywhere, and if the adults have more power they may actually be able to shield their magick from us so we won't know. It will help that Annisa and Landon have lived here their whole lives and will know if any new people are in town, but if they keep a low profile and aren't seen around town, then we won't know. The adults are not able to sense their magick if it is shielded like we can, so that won't help either. I don't think they will risk more than the two at the school, especially if they think their plan is working. I think they are going to keep as far a distance as they can until they are ready to make a move."

My dad furrows his brow before he expresses his next thought. "I think you may be taking this farther than it needs to be, and that the kids at your school were sent to keep an eye on you. I don't think there's any big plan or plot against you. Annisa and Landon are not used to not being the center of attention, and it's making you blow this out of proportion. I understand that the Council is still a threat, and they are trying to get the witches to rally against you, but I don't think that is what is happening right now. I think the witches decided to do some research for themselves and sent someone to watch, see how you were behaving, and to see if you are a real threat or not. The rest of what is going on at the school is still fallout from the beginning of the year. Teenagers are fickle. One minute you are the queen bee, and the next you are at the bottom of the pile."

I can tell from the expressions on all of the adults' faces

that they agree with him. I don't believe that's what is going on, but I have no proof, and no way to show them they are wrong. I can tell from the expressions on Landon, Chase, and Penelope's faces, that they think the same thing I do. It looks like for the first time, we are not on the same page as our parents. We know we will not be able to convince them they are wrong about this. We are on our own. It isn't long before the adults go upstairs and head to their separate homes to get ready for bed. We stay in the secure room a little longer.

Chase waits for the door to close. "I think they aren't willing to accept that our own people would turn against us. They are holding onto the belief that we are connected, and our main focus is to help people, so strongly, that they won't see the truth of the situation until they have no other choice."

Penelope sighs. "We won't have their help or advice on this. We are going to have to keep quiet about this so they don't try to stop us from doing anything they don't like. I know they are trying to protect us, but they don't see the whole picture."

We agree that there is nothing that we can do about it until we have more information. We go to bed that night feeling more than a little lost.

CHAPTER 4

The next few weeks at school are the same. Fewer people talk to us, and it is becoming clear that we are becoming the people at school that everyone else avoids. Cheerleading and football practice are getting more difficult as the squad and team are turning hostile towards us. The coaches finally pull Landon, Penelope, and I off to the side to talk to us. The two coaches exchange worried looks before the cheerleading coach begins. "I hate to bring this up, but we really don't have a choice in the matter anymore. I don't know what it was that you did, but we have gotten complaints from every member on the squad and football team that they don't feel like you are suitable for the captain positions."

I look over at Penelope. If we are just being demoted, Penelope would not be in this conversation. The coach notices my look and sighs. "It is not just the captain positions. It has been brought to our attention that both the cheerleading squad and the football team no longer feel comfortable working with you three. For some reason, which we still haven't figured out, because nobody will give a definite reason, they don't want you three on the squad or the team anymore. Normally, we let these teenager squabbles play themselves out, but it has been going on for quite a while now and they are refusing to participate unless you three are removed. I'm sorry, but it looks like we're going to have to cut you from the squad and the team."

I have tears streaming down my face. Chase sees them, and runs over to find out what is going on. He hears the last of the announcement about us being cut. He gives the coaches a glare. "You are going to let a bunch of whiney spoiled kids tell you how to run your teams? You know that these three are the best on the squad and team."

I put my hand on his arm and shake my head. It isn't going to work to get us back on, and even if it does, what kind of squad or team would we be if everyone else refuses to participate? Chase gives the coaches a nasty look, wraps his arms around me and hugs me close until I'm done crying. When I look up, I see that Landon has done the same for Penelope, but he has a weird look on his face. I realize the only thing Landon has is football. He has us and our magick, but the only thing he has for himself, is football. He takes a great deal of pride in the fact that he is good at being captain and quarterback. It is different for him than the rest of us. I am upset, but it doesn't collapse my world. Landon can't say that. I am really glad that he has Penelope to help him through this. She is upset about being cut from the squad, but since this is the first time that she has been on a squad, it isn't something that she can't get over in a few days or weeks.

As I realize the impact that this is having on Landon, I go from being upset and self-pitying to angry. I am angry at the new kids. I know that this is their doing, I just can't figure out how. How are two new kids, who have only known these other kids for a few weeks, getting them to turn their backs on us? How are they able to come into our lives and completely destroy everything we have worked for? What gives them the right to do this to us? We haven't done anything wrong. We haven't hurt anybody that wasn't trying to kill us. We stayed in our little town, and minded our own business, and they think they can just waltz in here and destroy our lives? I won't let them!

Chase can feel the turn in my emotions, so he pulls back a little bit taking in my expression. He takes a step back at the anger I let show in my eyes. I take that opportunity to turn away from him and stalk back to the school. I am so angry that even if everyone wasn't trying to avoid me they would have gotten out of my way to let me pass because of the look on my face. My anger doesn't get the outlet I want. The new kids are already gone from the school. I look everywhere they might be, and I get angrier the longer I search. Chase follows behind me and doesn't say anything. Landon and Penelope have already left to go back to Landon's house.

When we get back in the car to head back to my house Chase keeps glancing at me. I am still extremely angry, so this annoys me even more. I ignore it until we get to my house. When we get there and have settled in on the couch to watch some T.V. Chase finally breaks the silence. "Are you going to tell me why you're so pissed?"

I glare at him and he holds his hands up in surrender. "I am not trying to start a fight, I just want to know what is going on in that head of yours. I can tell by the murderous look on your face, and the anger in your emotions, but you are so pissed that I can't attempt to talk to you in your head. I don't think you would be able to hear me over the screaming that your own mind is doing."

I sigh and let go of some of the anger so I am able to have a reasonable conversation with him and not take it out on him. "I am upset about losing my spot on the squad. I worked hard to get to be captain and it was taken away from me for reasons that had nothing to do with me, or my ability to handle the position. If that was all it was, I would have been able to handle it. The thing that has me so pissed, is that football is all Landon has for himself. He has us, our magick and Penelope, but football is how he defines himself. He will be completely destroyed by this. I'm sure he will deal with it and move on, but it will take him a long time."

"And that is what caused you to stalk the hallways of the school looking for someone you could hurt?" He smirks as he leans back and crosses his arms over his chest.

"I wasn't looking for someone to hurt. I was looking for the new kids. It is their fault, and their influence, that is doing this. I can't figure out how they are making the kids we have known our whole lives turn their backs on us. I was looking for them so I could confront them and make them tell me what they are doing. Is it magick or is it just them starting rumors?" I stand up and start pacing trying to burn off the lingering anger.

Chase leans forward resting his arms on his knees. "You know, we really should figure out what their names are. We can't keep calling them the new kids."

I laugh at this. That is the response he was trying for. He smiles, catches me around the waist when I pass by him, and pulls me into his side so we can cuddle up on the couch and watch T.V. About an hour later Landon and Penelope show up. Landon walks in with his head hung low and Penelope stalks in just as pissed as I was earlier. Chase and I exchange a worried look as Landon sits on the loveseat and Penelope throws herself on the cushion next to him.

Penelope's anger is pouring off of her. "Please tell him football is not all he is. He seems to be under the impression that if he doesn't have football, he is useless. I am going to seriously hurt Brian and Amy for this." I look over at Chase with a look that shows how worried I am about this. As she finishes, Landon, Chase, and I all gawk at her completely confused. She scans our faces and laughs. "Did you guys seriously not know their names? Have you still been calling them the new kids?"

I shrug my shoulders. "Chase and I were just saying that we had to figure out what their names are."

Landon stares at us all in disbelief. "We have been thrown off the football team and cheerleading squad and you can sit here and joke?" He turns. "Annisa, we both worked really hard to get to where we are on the squad and team and we are really good at what we do. How are we supposed to just move on from that? Football is who I am. I don't know who I am without it."

I turn to him with sympathy in my eyes. "Landon, I understand that is how you feel, but it's not true. You have us and your magick. Football is something you enjoy doing, not who you are. You are the same person you were this morning. Football doesn't define you. You get to choose who you are. It's not decided by something you are good at."

Chase adds his opinion. "Look, dude, I know you had your pride trampled on, but you have to look at the big picture. You were great at being the captain of the team and the quarterback, but she's right. It's not who you are. You are great at strategy and control, and that is what made you so good on the team. I think the team is what gave you the skills you will need to deal with what we have coming our way. Honestly, I think it is a good thing you are not on the team anymore. Now we can focus on keeping everyone from being hurt. I understand it meant a lot to you, but it is just a game that teaches you what you have already learned."

When I was talking Landon was looking at me like he thought I was telling him what I thought he needed to hear. When Chase is done, Landon has a look on his face that shows that he believes what Chase had to say, and he will be able to move past this. Penelope has a triumphant look on her face when she realizes he is finally going to move to a new topic of conversation.

Landon looks around at us. "Thank you. It will take some time, but I think I will be able to get over this and move on. We need to focus on Brian and Amy, and figure out how they are doing this. I can't believe that people would turn their backs on us from some rumors. I can see them acting a little mean for a while, but nothing like what has been going on. It has to be some kind of spell."

I shake my head. "I was thinking the same thing, but that would take a great deal of power to cast a spell over that many people, and maintain it for this long. It would be impossible for someone to accomplish that."

Penelope puts her finger up to let us know she has an idea, but needs to get her thoughts in order before she can tell us. After a few minutes of silence, she looks up with an astonished look on her face. "I can't believe I didn't think about this sooner. What if it isn't a spell on them, but a spell on us? It would be possible for someone to cast and maintain a spell on the four of us instead of the school. All they would have to do is use a spell that affects the way that people see us. We would never feel the spell because it would be to glamour our look to others."

We look at each other shocked. She's right. We should have thought of that sooner. Chase is the first to overcome his shock at the realization, "How do we figure out if that is what is happening?"

I sigh. "Well, I don't think our parents would be willing to listen if we tell them our theory. I don't want to risk going to the woods and letting Brian and Amy know that there is something in that land either. We need to try and keep them away from it by not leading them there. They may be here to watch us, but that is not the only thing they are here to do. They are trying to distract us, and that is probably the reasoning behind the spell to begin with. Since we wouldn't feel it, they most likely think we will spend all of our time trying to get our influence back at the school."

Penelope eyes light up. "I agree. I think if we do find a way to break the spell that we shouldn't try to get our spots back. Landon, I know this is hard for you, but it really is best that we free up more of our time and try to throw them off their game a little."

Landon looks sad but agrees. "You're right. We need to shake their confidence and try to buy some time to figure out their long term plan. First, we need to break the spell. Then we need to lay low. If they think we are power hungry, not rising back up to power when the opportunity presents itself, should throw them off."

Chase stands up and motions for us to follow him out

into the back yard. "We don't know which element they used, or what they are strongest in, but we do know that we can also use whatever element they used, and that we are stronger. All we have to do is ask the elements to assist in removing any spells that have been cast on us."

Penelope looks nervous. "I'm not sure that's such a good idea. We don't know if our parents have placed any protection spells on us. They know more about the dangers of what we need to be protected from, and if we remove a spell they placed, we could be putting the whole town in danger. We also don't know if being in this area was on purpose. Maybe we are meant to be here to help protect the woods and the land where all magick originated. If there are any spells related to that, and we remove it, it could really do a lot more harm that we intend."

I hadn't thought about that. Our parents haven't really had an opportunity to fill us in on all that there is to do with our world, so there could very possibly be some spells they have cast on us that we know nothing about. After giving it some thought I make a different suggestion. "Maybe we just need to be more specific in what we ask the elements to remove. We don't know for sure if it was Brian and Amy who cast the spell, or someone else here that we don't know about, so we can't just ask to have their spells removed. We can ask for spells that were cast with the intention of harm be removed. I'm sure our parents wouldn't place a spell on us that was intended to cause harm, and any spell that is for the protection of the land would not be intended to harm us. We just have to be very specific to remove any spells that are intended to hurt us and us alone."

After some discussion on how the wording needs to be, we join hands, close our eyes and say the spell. "Earth, Air, Fire, and Water we ask for your assistance. Find the magick intended for harm to us and wash them away. As we four stand strong, blow, burn, drown, and bury all intentions of harm and negativity placed on us."

We didn't consider that our parents might have been

affected by the spell placed on us. When we walk into the house and see our parents looking at us with confused expressions, we realize we did not fail to convince them of our problems. They had been unable to see our problems the way that they were.

We move to the secure room. I am a little nervous about this conversation. "From the on your faces, I think you may have been affected by the same spell everyone at the school has been. Apparently, the kids on the football team and cheerleading squad talked the coaches into having us cut from the teams. We figured out we had a spell cast on us to influence how others saw us."

My mom still looks confused. "I don't understand what is going on. I have a lot of memories of us talking, but it's really foggy. I can't actually remember what the conversations were, or what any of us said. I can't see what it was or why I was so frustrated."

Penelope tries to explain. "We think that when Brian and Amy moved to town they placed a spell on us so that every time someone saw us they would think that we were either really bad people, or overreacting to something. It was designed to make people see us in a negative way. We were outside removing the spell and that is why you can't remember the conversations."

My dad looks impressed. "That is actually a great plan. You never would have felt the spell because it didn't hurt you or anyone else."

I frown at him. "Dad, are you seriously impressed with them doing a spell that caused us so much trouble?"

His face started to turn a little red. "Sorry, honey, but you have to admit, it was a good idea, and it was executed perfectly."

I scowl at him and move on. "Well, I guess we'll see how it goes tomorrow. We'll either still be hated, or everyone will be wondering what happened."

My mom gives me a sympathetic look. "It will work out one way or another."

CHAPTER 5

After Chase and I have gotten ready for bed, I go down to the kitchen to get a drink. I stop in the doorway to listen when I hear my mom talking. "We really need to tell them. They have a right to know."

I am really curious and even though I feel guilty about it, I stand outside the door and listen to my parent's conversation. My dad replies, "Yes, they need to know, just not yet. I don't think they are ready. They have enough to deal with and I refuse to add to that."

My mom groans in frustration. "Maybe you're right. I just wish we weren't the only ones that knew about this. It's impossible to know if knowing would help or hurt them. I guess we should probably wait and see if it's something critical to the situation before we decide on when to tell them."

My parents start to turn off the lights, so I quickly make my way back to my room as quietly as possible so they won't know I have been listening at the door. When I close the bedroom door, Chase can immediately tell that something is wrong. I tell him about the conversation that I overheard and wait for his response. After a few minutes he says, "I don't know what to think about that. It could be either bad or good. If the other adults don't know makes me think it can't be good. I don't know how we can get them to tell us before they are ready to either. It worries me that they are keeping something from us that sounds like it is really important."

"Without telling them that I was eavesdropping at the door and I know that they are keeping something from us, there is no way for us to even ask them about it. I will try to find a way to ask without letting them know that we know something."

"That is the best we can do for now. We have to trust that they will give us the information if it is something we need to know." He wraps he arms around me and holds me close.

We are both uncomfortable with the new situation, but we can't find a way out of it. Since there is really nothing that we can do about it right now, we go to bed. I still marvel at the fact that our parents have agreed to let us live together. Being soul mates means we feel like a piece of our soul is missing when we are not together. Instead they decided to let us live together rather risk one of us getting caught sneaking into each other's rooms at night by a neighbor and have to explain to the police what happened. I'm not sure why this thought floats through my mind as I drift off to sleep.

The alarm goes off and I roll over groaning. I am not ready to face another frustrating day. I just want to hide in bed. Chase chuckles and down pulls the covers that I had pulled up over my head. "You can't hide all day in bed. We have a lot to figure out, and a whole town that could be in danger."

I glare at him. "You are not allowed to lecture me before I have even gotten out of bed. I should have a period of grace where you are not allowed to remind me of how screwed up things are in the morning."

He laughs at me as he gets out of bed and heads to the

guest room to take a shower. I know that I can't put it off any longer, so I get out of bed and get ready to face the day and whatever it throws my way. When we get downstairs, everybody is here for breakfast. I am instantly on alert, we usually only meet like this for dinner.

My mom notices my hesitancy. "We just wanted to talk to you before you left for school. Don't worry, nothing is wrong. We are still the parents and we can gather you for parental advise from time to time. It doesn't have to be about some major life changing event. We just want to make sure you know how you want to handle the situation at school. The other kids are not going to understand what happened. They are going to have some memories of the last few weeks, but they are going to be foggy, and they won't be able to pinpoint anything specific. All their other memories will be fine, so it will be even more confusing for them when it is only the memories that have to do with you that they can't quite remember."

I sigh. "So, try to act like everything is normal and there was some kind of big blow up, but not give details. Got it. We can handle that. We have been dealing with the weird behavior for quite a while now, so that won't be too hard. We just have to remember it wasn't their fault. It was Brian and Amy's doing. Before you say it, yes we know not to confront them at school. Hopefully, the other kids will finally be able to see them for what they are now. Is there anything else that we need to know?"

My mom glances at dad. "What do you mean?"

"Just making sure we have all the information that we need. I don't want to walk into a situation not knowing everything." I raise a brow in challenge.

Chase rolls his eyes at me. My dad doesn't notice. "Nope, you know what we know."

I look at Chase frustrated. There is nothing more I can do without saying I overheard their conversation and know that they aren't telling us something. We finish breakfast and leave for school. When we pull up, we sit in the car for a few minutes. We are afraid to get out of the car and see what is waiting for us. We are not prepared for what we walk into.

As soon as we walk into the school, we notice Brian and Amy are uncharacteristically standing off to the side with smirks on their faces. The smirks disappear quickly when they notice everyone else is looking at us with confused expressions. Everyone knows we are no longer on the football team or the cheerleading squad, but they can't remember what actually happened. Brian and Amy seem to be figuring out that we have broken the spell and are watching closely for our reaction. We get ready for our first classes like nothing has happened.

The girl that replaced me as captain comes up as I am closing my locker. Chase is standing next to me and takes my hand to let me know that he is not going anywhere.

"I don't think it was the right decision to not have you as the captain. I was happy with the way you were running the squad. I don't remember what happened exactly, but I would really like it if you came back as captain."

I smile at her and try to look calm and collected, even though my heart is pounding in my chest, and my stomach is in knots. "I understand. It was all a big misunderstanding, but I think it's best I not come back for now. You will be great as captain. If you need any advice, feel free to come talk to me. I will be happy to help you, but I need some time away from cheerleading."

When she walks away I look up at Chase and he looks at me with sympathy. "I know that was hard, but I really think it is what is best right now."

"I know. It is the only reason I was able to turn her down. It doesn't make it any easier or lessen the disappointment." I confess. The rest of the day people keep coming up to us and saying they can't remember what happened, but they are glad we've worked it out, and they are sorry for anything they may have said or done to make matters worse. We continue with saying it was all a big misunderstanding and not giving any details.

As much as Brian and Amy had been trying to show they had no interest in us before, they are showing interest in us now. Every time we look around, we see them watching us. The more we thank people for the offers of coming back to the squad and team and we keep turning them down, the more confused they seem to be. I don't think they can figure out why we are content to be normal students and not at the top of the class.

After school, Landon looks like he is dealing with the whole situation a lot better than he was the day before. He confirms it when we get in the car. "It was really hard to turn the team down when they wanted me to come back. As the day went on, and I told more and more of them that I needed a break from the team, the more the decision felt right. I think you were right Chase, I have learned all I was meant to on the football team. I really liked the looks on Brian and Amy's faces when we didn't do what they expected."

Penelope laughs. "It was a great satisfaction after everything they have put us through to see them fall on their faces. I know it's mean, but I really liked that the other kids couldn't remember why they liked them so much. It was like they had to start all over again, but since they weren't taking our place or making it look like we were these horrible people it wasn't as easy this time."

I have to agree, but there is still something bothering me. "I liked seeing them thrown off their game, but something didn't seem right about it. It was almost like they expected this to happen. I got the feeling they expected us to figure out the spell and break it. They were surprised we didn't immediately take our spots back, but I think they had anticipated that was a possibility too. It was as if they were studying us and already knew what was going to happen, they just needed to observe it to confirm what they already knew. I don't know why I get that feeling, but I do." We have gotten back to my house by this point and go down to the secure room to make sure that we aren't overheard.

When we are situated Chase says, "I got the same feeling.

I can't explain it either. I don't know if it is our instincts telling us, or something else. I hate to not trust our instincts, but if this is another spell I would hate to jump to conclusions that could hurt us later."

It seems Landon has been thinking about strategy during this whole conversation. "I don't think it is another spell. I think they know a lot more about us than we know about them, like almost everything there is to know about us. I feel like we are at a distinct disadvantage."

I look questioningly over at Chase. He nods his head to indicate he agrees. I need to tell them about what I overheard last night. While I am telling them about my parents' conversation, understanding shows on their faces. Penelope laughs. "I was wondering what that was about this morning, you asking if there was anything that we needed to know." She gets serious after that, "You don't think that it has anything to do with them knowing so much about us, do you?"

We exchange glances with each other, because none of us seem to have an answer. I know now that if my parents don't tell us we are going to have to just ask, and I am going to have to admit that I had been eavesdropping at the door. When they get home from work and realize that we are down in the secure room, they come down before they start dinner.

We tell them about what happened, and our theories. I watch my parents closely to see what their reaction will be. They exchange a worried glance. When we have finished and we look at them waiting for their response, my mom turns to my dad. "We have to tell them. They really need to know."

I can't take it anymore so I blurt out, "We know you are keeping something from us. I went downstairs to get a drink last night and heard you in the kitchen talking. I listened at the door."

My dad sighs. "That would explain the conversation this morning." He then looks at my mom. "You should be the one to tell them. You are better at explaining it."

CHAPTER 6

My mom looks really uncomfortable, avoiding eye contact by picking invisible lint off her pants, when she tells the other adults, who are completely confused by what is going on, "None of you know about this. We haven't told anyone, because it was not something anyone could do anything about." We wait for her to gather her thoughts and tell us what it is they know that the rest of us don't. I never would have thought what she has to say could change the way that I look at our new world or that I would feel that violated.

She looks around at everyone, sighs. She sits back in her seat defeated. "I'm sorry we didn't tell you about this sooner. We didn't figure this out until earlier in this lifetime. As there are two teenagers at the school, there are at least two families here, since only one child is allowed to each couple with the exception of Chase and Penelope. We believe those two families are linked, and it is not just them. We think there is a whole nest of them from a group of witches that have been advisors to the Council, but they have been working toward their own agenda since the beginning." The other adults gasp in surprise at this.

"If this group is the one that suggested to the Council that you four be created, they did research on the witches that were down here. They knew when the Council put you down here for your first life cycle, that your individual personalities would emerge, and anyone with that much power would have strong personalities. They were counting on the Council not being able to control you, and that you would turn on them. Unfortunately, they know everything there is to know about you, because they are the ones that provided the Council with the information to have you be created exactly the way they wanted you. We think they are the ones that have been casting the spells to make sure that you stayed within your punishment until they were ready to use you against the Council."

We are shocked by this, but the most important question had yet to be addressed.

"Why would they do this? The answer is simple. If you destroy the Council, they think they can take control and be the ones in charge. By making it look like you are the bad guys, they can swoop in and save everyone it sounds similar to what the Council is trying to do, but it has vastly different results."

We sit, lost in our own thoughts for a few minutes before Chase asks, "How do you know this, and why did you think it was information that we wouldn't need?"

My dad answers this time. He leans forward in his seat. "We didn't know for sure it was the same group. We thought it was, but until we knew for sure, it wouldn't have done anyone any good to have something else to worry about. We found out by accident. I was doing some research and came across a link that took me to information they had collected. Since they are spread out and move around frequently, they keep their files online. Me being a programmer, I can hack into files. I know it's wrong, but from what I've seen, it is information we need to know. For example, they weren't expecting us to be split up this time. It made them have to move their plans up. When they weren't able to find all of you and cast the spells, you were able to break free from your punishment before they were ready for you to."

I feel completely violated. I can't sit still after hearing this. I stand up and start to pace. These people have manipulated not only this life cycle, but every life cycle I have ever lived. Coercing me into doing exactly what they had planned. What is worse, is they have been watching us, and taking notes about how we react to different situations as if we are lab rats. As angry and violated as I feel, I know this is not the right time to dwell on these feelings. There is so much more we need to discuss now that we know.

I want to make sure that I understand the whole thing correctly. "So basically, this group of people manipulated the Council into creating us so they could use us to overthrow the Council, and we would take the fall? And, the Council is playing right into their hands by trying to make it look like we are trying to overthrow them because we are power hungry."

My mom looks defeated. She starts to twist her hair between her fingers as she watches me pace. "That about sums it up. Now that we know this, and we look back at the whole thing, we can see where they imposed their influence to make sure the situation went in the way that would benefit them the most. I know this is hard to deal with. You have had so much thrown at you lately. At least now that we know what they are up to, it will be easier to figure out what to do next."

Landon is not happy about the situation as his jaw clenches and his fists tighten, but I can tell he feels the same way as I do, that it's not the right time to deal with the anger and violation. "How many people are in this group exactly? We need to know what we are dealing with here."

I know it is probably wrong, but I actually feel better knowing we are not the only ones who were being kept in the dark. Judging by the looks on their faces, the other adults do not feel the same way as I do. It looks like they are pretty upset that my parents had not shared this information with them. They must also feel it is not the right time to talk about it, but I have a feeling they will be talking about it later with my parents, who are avoiding everyone's eyes.

My dad answers Landon's question as he leans back in his chair again. "From the information I was able to get, it looks like there are three families, so six adults and three teenagers. You probably won't recognize any of them. From their note they have always been careful to make sure that none of us actually saw them while they were watching us. I am starting to wonder if the parents sent the kids here by themselves since we haven't encountered the parents. In a town as small as this, it would be almost impossible for nobody to have seen them. Of course, we can't just go around asking about them either. We don't want to let on that we know.

My best guess is that two families are here, and the other one is traveling to make sure others believe the rumors while placing enough doubt so nobody will come here looking for you, yet. They want to make them suspect you, but don't want to take the chance of something going wrong. I think they are trying to buy time hoping the Council will get tired of waiting and will make a move to force your hand."

Everything my dad is saying makes sense. There is still one thing that is really worrying me. "What about the power in the land? If they know about how this started, they must know the ancient magick is here."

My mom is shaking her head. "The ancient magick is a power that nobody can completely control. It chooses who it lets wield it, and who it allows to know it is there. It seems to have chosen you four as its Guardians. The only reason you remember what you do, is because it allows it. It helped you defeat Peter because of this. For most witches, they will never feel comfortable in the area close to that land. You feel comfortable and welcome because the magick calls to you. You feel protective of it, because that is the way it wants it."

I look around at the others. They have the same shocked look on their faces that I do. We didn't know that. So many in our world are looking for this place, it never occurred to us that the ancient magick is protecting itself. Penelope runs her hands through her long black hair and looks at us with her bright blue eyes that are the same shade as Chase's. I can tell that she is frustrated by the look in her eyes, "So, we are not only supposed to save our world from the corruption of the Council, and this new group, but also protect the land that has the most powerful and sought after magick too?"

The other adults have either gotten over being kept in the dark, or decided to push it to the side for now. Landon's mom adds "I know it sounds overwhelming. You have to remember that nobody knows about the power in the land. They know there is a place of power here, but they think it is like the other places of power in other parts of the world. They will not likely seek it out, because they don't believe it will be able to boost their magick enough to make it worth it to limit their area of practice. Nobody realizes it is here, and the ancient magick is keeping it that way. Having you here is an extra precaution."

I am still confused about how this whole thing works. I stop pacing and perch on the edge of my chair. "So, if the ancient magick keeps itself cloaked, how did the Council know to start us there?"

Landon's dad speaks up. As a historian, he has researched this area before. He clears his throat before he begins. "You are misunderstanding how we came to be. The Council was created by the ancient magick to be a governing entity over the magickal beings that the ancient magick was creating to help the lives of the other beings already living on the planet. There was so much struggling, and the ancient magick is about balance. Most of the time, the balance between good and bad was close, but when negativity started to pull ahead, something had to be done. Because of this balance, we had to be created with the ability to decide for ourselves. If we were created with the inability to do anything bad, it would have shifted the balance too far in the direction of good.

The Council was supposed to be somewhat of an exception. They would still have the choice, but the ancient magick intended to remain a guiding force to keep them fair. The problem is, the more powerful the Council got, the less they listened to what the ancient magick was trying to tell them. That is when the corruption started. They started to see what they could accomplish to make themselves the most powerful and feared beings in existence."

Chase has been quiet through all of this. He has been staring at the floor listening but now he looks up with a furrowed brow. "We need to make sure we listen to what the ancient magick is trying to tell us. If we try to do things the way our impulses or emotions tell us, we could actually make things worse. We felt that power when we were fighting Peter. It was pure, and it guided us when we weren't sure what to do. I think that is what we were feeling when we figured out that Brian and Amy knew a lot more than they were saying. The ancient magick was guiding us. I think it would be best for us to listen to that from now on, and not question it."

Penelope rolls her eyes at him. "We can't just blindly do whatever it is we feel like doing. We have to make sure we are being guided and not under a spell or following our emotions first. It's going to take time to figure out what the guidance feels like so we don't mistake it for something else."

I raise my eyebrows. "I hadn't thought about that. With us connected the way we are, we could easily take an emotion we are strongly feeling and mistake that for the guidance of the ancient magick. I didn't notice anything different in the feelings I was getting from Brian and Amy, just that I couldn't say why I felt them."

Landon has been following along with the conversation. "I think it will just take time to figure out the feeling. I'm sure it feels different, but we weren't looking for that, we were only looking for a justification of the feeling. The first thing we need to do when we are feeling something we can't explain is look at the emotions the rest of us are experiencing.

If the feeling that we should do something in particular doesn't fit in with what any one of us is feeling, we can look deeper to see where it is coming from. If it is from the ancient magick, it will let us know. I think it is trying to help us. We didn't know to listen to it. For example, Annisa, why didn't you just get a drink out of the bathroom instead of going downstairs to get a glass of water?"

I am shocked. "I don't know. I didn't even think about it. I just went downstairs because I wanted a glass of water. I see what you mean though."

The stress of the situation is showing in Landon's twitching jaw, Penelope wringing her hands, Chase leaning over with his elbows on his knees as he taps his foot and my constantly fidgeting with my hair. I take in the signs and voice my concern. "I think we need to call it a night. We are tired and stressed. We should get some rest and talk about it later."

CHAPTER 7

The next day at school, we study Brian and Amy. If they know so much about us, then we need to know as much as we can find out about them. Maybe, if we see the way they react to different situations, we might be able to get an idea of how they would react in a fight. None of us have any classes with them in the mornings, so our opportunities are limited. It is easier to get more information on Brian, with three of us that can watch him. Penelope has to get the bulk of the information on Amy, since they are a year behind the rest of us.

After school we meet in the secure room to discuss what we learned. Penelope starts since she has the least amount of information. "I don't know what you want to know, she has red hair and hazel eyes, she seems to pay attention in class, and she doesn't make a scene or throw fits. She is just an average teenager. She does have a tendency to flirt with the cute boys, and likes the attention she gets from them. One thing that bugs me, is that she always positions herself so she can watch me, no matter who she is talking to, or what she is doing. I hadn't noticed that before. She doesn't watch me fully so that everyone can tell that's what she is doing, but she always keeps me in her periphery. It made it difficult to watch her, when she was always watching me."

I give her a sympathetic look. "I know what you mean. Whenever I was around Brian I had the same problem. He has sandy blonde hair and brown eyes, he doesn't really flirt with the girls, but he does like getting attention from them. He plays the shy new guy to get them to come to him. Most of the girls are eating that up. Most of the other guys aren't shy, so this is completely new for the girls in our school. They are used to outgoing and everybody knowing everything about them. He is getting a lot of attention from the girls. He is also always positioned so that he could keep me in his sight."

Landon and Chase both roll their eyes at me. Chase laughs. "I'm so glad that what you noticed was how much attention he was getting from the other girls and what color his hair and eyes were."

It is my turn to roll my eyes at him. He looks at the others. "He is not using the shy guy routine to get the girls to flock to him. He is using it so he can hide behind them. Even though all the girls know that I am taken, they still flirt a little bit with me." He looks over at me to see my reaction to this.

I am a little upset he didn't tell me about it, but I understand why. I also don't mind that they do. I trust him and know that nothing will come of it, and if it makes them feel better, who is it really hurting?

Seeing that I am not going to blow up at his statement he continues. "He takes advantage of this. I am confident and never let them think they have even the slightest chance with me. When they walk away a little disappointed, he is an easy target to boost their egos back up. He makes it seem like he is so lucky they even notice him, let alone talk to him. He makes sure that he's positioned where, when the girls walk away from me, he is the first one they see. It would be a good plan of action if that was actually what he was trying for. To everyone else, well the guys anyway, that is what it looks like he is doing. That alone shows that he is very intelligent and manipulative. He is able to put out an appearance that puts him in the light he wants to be seen in, while he is doing something that nobody would approve of."

Landon has been nodding his head in agreement. "I agree. I thought maybe I was reading too much into his behavior. Since you have given the same description that I would have, I have to believe that is what's going on. It makes me wonder what he is really like. Which brings me to my next idea, what do you think about us getting to know them better?"

We look at him like he has grown a second head. He laughs and continues. "It would be a good idea to know our enemies. We don't know if they have been fed a line that they have had no reason to doubt, or if they really feel this is the way it should be. I am sure they are just as curious about how we really are as we are of them. We should try and be friends with them. Maybe we can convince them what they have been led to believe all this time is not true. Since they are our age, and we don't start to get our memories until we turn 16, they are starting to get their memories too. We still have time to let them see that maybe they were wrong about us. We can attempt to show them we are not power hungry. We might be able to convince them, as they have never been given the option to form their own opinion."

He makes sense. I don't like it, but he has a really good point. "I can't think of a valid argument to that. I don't trust them, but that is not a good enough reason."

Penelope has been quiet through all of this. "We need to listen to our instincts on this one. I can feel that there is a way we should handle this, but I can't put my finger on it."

I'm not sure I can trust my feelings on this. I am very undecided on what we should do. Both Landon and Penelope make good points. I am not sure why but Landon's idea sounds like a good one. When I concentrate on trying to make a decision I feel a guiding hand showing me where it wants me to go. I finally recognize the guiding hand as the ancient magick. I focus on the feeling so it will be easier to recognize in the future. When I look up, I can tell by the looks on their faces, the others have figured it out as well.

Chase doesn't look happy. "Alright, looks like we are making friends with the people who are working against us. I still don't trust them, and I don't think we should give them any important information."

Penelope rolls her eyes. "Nobody is saying we need to go camping or share all of our secrets with them. We will have to let them get to know the real us if we have any hope of this working though. We can't just keep ourselves shut off from them if we have any hope of convincing them that we are not power hungry witches with an agenda of total domination. I also think we need to keep it a secret that we can talk in each other's heads, it would make matters worse if they know about how strong our bond is."

Chase looks over at her irritated. "I think we are all smart enough to know not to reveal that important detail."

I can tell Landon is getting ready to step in to defend Penelope. I interrupt him to try to keep an argument from happening. "Ok, we know that we are stressed, and as amusing as your sibling bickering is, we really need to finish this discussion." I put a hand on Chase's arm to try and calm his irritation. I turn to Landon. "Don't try to get in the middle of it, you will just make it worse. They are brother and sister, and they are going to bicker. I just try to keep from laughing and let it play out on its own." I laugh so they know that I'm sincere. They laugh too and the tension in the room is gone as quickly as it came.

Penelope gives Chase a glare and continues with what she was trying to say. "Obviously, I will try to make friends with Amy since I have her in a few of my classes, but what about Brian?"

We exchange glances. It takes a few minutes before Landon makes a suggestion. "Since this whole plan was my idea, I should be the one who approaches Brian."

I shake my head. "I don't think so. I think he would see it as a challenge if you approached him. I think it should be Chase. I would say me, but that would just open a whole can of worms about me trying to snag the new guy, and I think that would work against us right now. Chase is not in the position that you are at school. I don't mean that to sound bad for either one of you, but the fact is Landon, you are the guy every other guy in the school wants to be. Chase is the new guy. It would be natural for him to reach out to the only other new guy."

Chase is looking at me with a weird expression on his face. "I didn't think you realized how intimidating it was to walk into a school where everybody had known each other forever. If we were normal, then yes, I probably would have reached out to Brian on his first day at the school."

I narrow my eyes at him. "I may have never been on the other end of this. I may have grown up in this small town where everybody knows everyone else, but that does not mean that I am so self-centered that I don't know what it would be like for someone coming into this situation"

Landon and Penelope laugh and Chase pulls me onto his lap. I try to push away, but he holds onto me and won't let me up. "I was not trying to say that you are self-centered. I was surprised you knew what that would be like, since you never experienced it yourself."

I understand what he is saying and my anger dissipates, but I am not ready to let him off the hook yet. I pout. "You still thought I never thought about what you had gone through."

He can tell by my pout that I'm not really mad anymore and that I am just dragging it out. He starts tickling me to get back at me. When Penelope and Landon are laughing so hard they have tears streaming down their faces, Chase finally lets up. Now that we have relieved some stress, we are able to get back to the discussion. Just as we are getting ready to start talking about it again, our parents walk in. Penelope's mom instantly sees our red eyes and immediately thinks something is wrong.

"What happened? Why do you have red puffy eyes like you have been crying?"

The parents look at us with worried expressions. This is too much for us and we start laughing again. When we are finally able to get ourselves under control again, we explain about the stress relieving tickling that I had undergone and had everyone laughing so hard they were crying. Relief washes over each of their faces. They find seats and listen as we tell them about what we have found out and what our plan is.

My mom shakes her head. "Sometimes it still amazes me how mature you four are. We have always seen you acting like the teenagers that you are. This time it is hard to see you act so grown up. It's difficult to believe that you aren't little kids anymore, then you go and do something like this and we can't deny it."

The dads roll their eyes, and the other two moms look at her with understanding in their eyes. Penelope and Chase's mom says, "I am glad they were able to get to this point and be themselves this time. I am still having a hard time with them being so grown up though. I hated not having them grow up together this time, it was always us that was a big family. This time we didn't have that. Since this is the result, I can't bring myself to regret that decision anymore. It seems to have strengthened their bond instead of making it harder for them to bond like we feared."

Landon's mom agrees. "It was hard to not have you with us and to see Chase and Penelope growing up, but I knew it was harder for you since you were out there on your own. We at least had each other."

We listened with amazement as we realize the sacrifices our parents have made for us to be able to get where we are. We discuss the plan to try and befriend Brian and Amy for a little bit longer, then we go upstairs to eat dinner. It has been a long couple of days so we order a pizza and spend the rest of the night playing games.

CHAPTER 8

When we walk in the next day, we smile at Brian and Amy in the hallway before school starts. After lunch we can put our plan into action. We want them to think that we genuinely want to get to know them. I'm sure they aren't going to trust us any more than we trust them, but hopefully, we will be able to get past that. After school I am surprised to see Brian and Amy walking to the car with Chase and Penelope. I thought it would take a couple of days before they would chance being with the four of us at the same time, and that it would take at least a week before they trusted us enough to go somewhere with us.

Chase gives me a smirk when they all walk up. "I invited Brian and Amy to join us for shakes at the diner."

I smile at them. "Ok, sounds great. Do you guys have a car or do you need a ride?"

They look a little nervous and not sure what to think about me just agreeing without asking any questions. Brian replies suspiciously, "I have a car, we can meet you there. Is it the same place where all the kids hang out?"

Landon walks up. "Yeah. Best pizza in town."

Amy jumps. She didn't notice Landon walk up. A second later she has a scowl on her face. I assume it is because she doesn't like that he was able to sneak up on her and she wasn't aware of her surroundings.

Landon smiles. "Hi, my name is Landon Harris."

Amy rolls her eyes at him. She is snarky when she responds. "We know who you are. It's impossible to not know who you are in this school. I'm Amy Williams, and this is Brian Leeman."

I laugh at the stunned look on Landon's face. He is not used to girls talking to him like that. I think it is good for him, but keep that thought to myself. Chase on the other hand, can't resist the opportunity to give his best friend a hard time. "Will you look at that? There is a girl in this school who doesn't worship the ground that you walk on? I didn't think that would ever happen." Chase laughs as he moves out of the way so Landon can't get a good position to hit him on the arm. After the guys have stopped trying to hit the other one without getting hit themselves, and Penelope and I stop laughing so hard our stomachs are starting to hurt, we decide we need to get going before there aren't any tables left.

When we arrive it is pretty packed. It is Friday, so most of the students have made their way over here already. We manage to find a table with enough seats for six and we sit down. After deciding what we want, Landon goes to the counter and put in our orders. When he gets back, he looks over at Brian and Amy and decides to try and get some information, "How do you guys like our little town?"

Amy seems like she is withdrawn and not really wanting to get involved with our conversation, but Brian doesn't seem to have a problem talking to us. He has a look in his eyes like this is something he has been dreaming about. It occurs to me he has been watching and studying us for many life times and he is just now getting the chance to find out information straight from the source.

"It's a little intimidating at first. The kids seem nice

enough. There are not the same cliques that there are at other schools. It's just hard to get involved in a conversation when it revolves around something that happened with everyone there except for you, and it was so long ago that they each have a different version of what happened." He taps his fingers nervously on the table.

I laugh. "I can see where that would be a problem. There really aren't enough of us to form the usual cliques. Chase and Penelope were the first new students we've had in years, so none of us are used to having someone around that hasn't always been there. We tend to forget that not everybody knows everything that has ever happened to us."

I don't focus my attention on Brian, but on both of them. I don't want Amy to think that I am only talking to Brian. I can see some jealousy starting to show in her eyes, so I take a chance and ask the next question. I hope it will help the tension to get this out of the way first. "Are you two soul mates?"

Brian looks surprised that I would ask something like that, and in a crowded pizza place. Amy looks suspicious, but she has looked like that since we first sat down, so I have no way of knowing if it is her normal expression or if she really doesn't trust us. She is the one to answer. "Yes we are. We figured it out in the beginning and have never had a problem with anyone trying to come between us. We're really good together." I can hear the implications in her voice. I can tell she believes everything that has been told to her. The look Brian is giving her tells me that he doesn't. He has an open mind, and wants to make a decision about us for himself.

I smile and pretend that I don't catch on that she is insulting me. "Chase and I are soul mates, and so are Landon and Penelope. We weren't lucky enough to figure it out right away though. I'm glad you guys didn't have to go through what we did. I wouldn't wish that on anybody." I hope that my being open about it, will help release some of the tension. It seems to work. Amy has lost some of the suspicion from her eyes, and is now looking at me with some interest. Like she is considering the idea that maybe, just maybe, there is more to us than she has been told.

Brian is watching her to see her reaction. I can tell he wants to get to know us and make his own decision. His expression makes it seem like Amy has no intention of changing her mind about us.

Penelope tries a new approach. "You guys got here at a good time of year, we have nice weather and you don't have long until school is out for the summer. Do you have plans for vacations or anything like that?"

Amy continues to watch and observe. Brian rolls his eyes at her. "No, we are not planning any vacations this summer. We need to get settled in here. Since our parents just started new jobs, they can't get away right now."

Penelope continues. "What do your parents do?"

Amy looks uncomfortable about where the conversation is headed, but she doesn't say anything. Brian doesn't seem to mind answering. "My dad is an architect, and my mom is an artist. Amy's dad is a car salesman and her mom is a psychologist. What do your parents do?"

"Mine and Chase's dad is a banker and our mom is a librarian. Annisa's dad is a computer programmer and her mom is a realtor. Landon's dad is an historian and his mom is a lawyer. My dad's work had us moving a lot, but it wasn't bad because we got to see a lot of the country. Thankfully, this is his last transfer. They told him now that he is at the main branch, they will keep him here until he is ready to retire. Mom has always loved books, and it made sense for her to be a librarian because she could do that anywhere dad was transferred to."

Amy looks really surprised that Penelope is offering up so much information. Brian is just soaking everything up. I have a feeling he has wanted to be able to sit down and pick our brains and see how we think and what motivates us for a very long time. I am just glad the conversation is staying in the safe zones and we are able to give our answers without looking like we are trying to decide how much we want to reveal.

Landon cuts in abruptly. "What kind of art does your mom do?"

Brian gives him a funny look. "She paints. She has been successful in selling quite a few pieces to a gallery in New York. They really like her work up there."

I can tell that Brian is confused by Landon's fascination. I laugh. "Landon's mom has an explanation for everything that she does. The thought of sitting down and just creating a painting because she enjoyed it would never enter her mind. Landon is easily fascinated with people who are not so controlled and don't analyze every move before they make it."

Landon glares at me. He has always been a little annoyed that I find his fascination amusing. Brian looks horrified at the idea. "I couldn't imagine living life so planned out, or what it must have been like to have a lawyer for a mom. My mom is very laid back and lets me experience things on my own. She would try to guide me when I was headed in a direction that wasn't good for me, but other than that, I was pretty free to make my own decisions."

Landon looks like he is trying to imagine what that would be like. "My mom is very structured. She has to think about the consequences of every action before she does anything. I was still free to make my own decisions, but only after she had thoroughly explained the consequences of each choice. It didn't matter which way I was thinking about going, I had to hear the consequences of each action I could possibly take. It was exhausting. I finally learned not to ask her advice unless it was about something very important."

Amy looks like she can't take it anymore and has to contribute to the conversation. "It would have been great to just hear about the consequences. I also had to hear about the possible impact on me. My mom analyzes everything and everybody. As she would explain the possible consequences of each action, she would also add the possible mental issues that could be related to each consequence. I was just lucky that I had Brian to rescue me when she really got on a roll."

We laugh at that. I can tell she realizes she has revealed more than she had intended to. It looks like she is struggling with a decision. I can see the conflict in her eyes. I have a feeling her mother has probably warned her about the possible mental issues that could be attached to trusting someone you know you shouldn't. We sit and talk for a couple of hours and then decide to call it a night.

When we get back to our house, we make our way down to the secure room. As soon as everybody has found a seat I look around. "We used to sit in the living room or dining room to talk. I think we spend more time down here than anywhere else in the house now." Everyone else is shocked for a moment when they realize I am right. I shrug my shoulders and move on. "Ok, that is not important, just an observation. We had a nice dinner and a pretty good time with Brian and Amy tonight. Brian seems like this is an opportunity he has been waiting a long time for, and like he wants to make his own decision about us, but has never been given the chance to before now. Amy on the other hand, seems to believe everything she has been told about us. I don't think she is ready to admit that there is more to the story than she knows. I'm sure as they get more of their memories she will understand, but I don't know if either of them really knows much more. I think they have both been kept in the dark and have never been told the whole story."

Chase nods. "I think you're right. There would have been no reason for them to be told the whole story. It was their parents that started the whole thing, and since they planned on being the ones to use us when it was time, they never would have told them the whole plan. I think Brian and Amy have only been told that they need to watch so that everyone can be prepared to fight against us when we make our move."

Landon and Penelope are nodding their heads in agreement. My mom voices her opinion. "I think you guys have a pretty good handle on this. You should continue getting to know them, and letting them get to know you.

Don't expect them to fight against their parents when the time comes though. It was a fluke that Rayne was willing to help you. That won't happen this time. They might not fight against you, but they won't fight against them either.

CHAPTER 9

I wake up late. I find Chase in the living room and snuggle up close to him on the couch. He leans over and gives me a kiss. "I didn't want to wake you up. You haven't been sleeping well and needed the rest."

"Thank you. I didn't plan on sleeping this late. We don't really have anything that needs to be done I guess it was a good day to sleep in."

"How about we go on a date tonight? We haven't had much time for just the two of us lately. Nothing big and fancy, just dinner and a movie."

"That sounds great. It will be nice to be normal teenagers for the night." I smile up at him, but look away when Penelope and Landon walk in.

They sit on the loveseat and Penelope asks, "You guys don't have anything planned for us tonight do you? We were thinking about going to play goofy golf and go for a late dinner."

I laugh, "It seems like our minds all work in the same way. We were planning on going to dinner and a movie tonight."

We spend the day just hanging out at the house and watching T.V. We really should be doing some research or working on our magick. We just want to take a break from the stress of our situation for the day.

We see Brian and Amy are sitting just a few tables away at the same café we go to for dinner. They are in the middle of a very intense conversation and don't see us come in and sit down. I know it is wrong, but I listen to their conversation anyway. I figure if it is that intense, then it has to be about us. Self-centered I know, but I am right. Amy is the one talking at first. "You can't possibly believe they are not as bad as we have been told. They are just manipulating you."

"You don't know that. All any of us have ever done is study them from afar. None of us has ever taken the time to get to know them. How do we know what we are seeing is not taken out of context? Maybe there is a good reason for what they have done."

"What could possibly have been the reason for them to kill Peter? They could have restrained him and let the Council deal with his punishment like they were supposed to. They didn't. They took matters into their own hands and killed him because they didn't like what he was doing."

Chase has the same uncomfortable look on his face that I can feel on mine. We know the Council sent Peter to kill us, thus we could not turn him over to the Council for punishment. The problem is, the rest of our world thinks Peter came after us because of a misguided notion that Chase was his daughter's soul mate. They all think he was acting on his own accord this time, not the Council's orders.

Brian isn't convinced. "How do we know there wasn't more to that story? Why would he a believe so strongly that Chase was meant for Rayne, unless someone convinced him? I know you think Rayne convinced him, but who convinced Rayne? You know the strong pull, and the intense feelings we have for each other. How could she have thought Chase was her soul mate if she never had those feelings?"

After a few minutes Amy has an answer. "If she had

never found her soul mate, she wouldn't know how intense the feelings really are. She felt attraction to Chase and that is what she thought the feelings were about. Until you actually meet your soul mate, nobody can explain the connection or the feeling attached to that."

Brian concedes the point. "Ok. I'll agree with that. I still think there is more to that story than we know. I have been watching our parents. They are keeping things from us. They exchange long looks, and they stop to consider what they want to tell us. They are careful with how they reveal information. I don't see the harm in getting to know them. I think it will help our cause. If we know how they think, and how they interact with each other, we will have a better idea how to stop them if they really are trying to take over. After the other day, I'm not convinced that is what they are doing."

Amy is getting more frustrated. "If getting to know them would help, then we would have done it before now. Our parents would have told us to do it instead of warning us against it, and basically saying to stay away from them. There are reasons they want us not to have direct contact."

"What if the reason is that they are completely different than what we have always been told? What if our parents don't want us to figure out that they have been leading us in the way they want us to go, and not the way that is best for everyone?"

"Why would they do that? All we have ever done is try to protect our kind. We find the information, give it to those that need it to keep ourselves hidden, and to make sure that things run smoothly. The Council is our governing entity and our parents have always done everything they can to help them. Why would they make everyone believe these four are a major threat if it wasn't true?"

"I know you don't want to hear this, but I am going to say it anyway. Our parents are power hungry. You have heard the conversations they have when they think we aren't listening. They think the Council is old fashioned, and not current in what is going on now. They want to replace them.

They believe they can do a better job since they have spent so many lifetimes watching, and researching, all the witches. The problem is, they can't do that without creating a situation that allows them to look like the good guys when they take over."

Amy lets out an exasperated breath. "Don't start with that again. I told you that you were taking what was said out of context. You didn't hear the whole conversation. For all you know, they were talking about what those four are probably thinking."

With that she looks around the café and sees that we are there. Chase and I have been pretending not to listen to them, so it is easy to act like we are in the middle of a conversation of our own. A few minutes later, they pay their bill and leave. Amy gives us a suspicious look over her shoulder as they walk past us.

When they are gone, I let out a breath I didn't realize I've been holding. "That was close. I think she suspects we were listening. But, I'm sure that she would think that no matter what. She really doesn't like, or trust, us at all."

"At least Brian is not just blindly following along. I think Amy will eventually come around, she values his opinions and listens to him. She may argue, but she doesn't automatically dismiss what he says as not being possible. She is giving him the chance to prove to her that she is wrong."

"I hope you're right. I don't want this to come between them. I know they are completely different, but they do seem really good together. I know we don't always agree, but this is a pretty big issue for them to be on opposite sides of."

Chase just shakes his head at me. "One of them is trying to convince the other one that we are evil, and trying to take over the world, and you are worried about how their relationship will survive? Sometimes, I don't understand how that brain of yours works."

I stick my tongue out at him. "We need to get going if we are going to make it to the movie on time."

When we get to the movie theater, Brian and Amy are ahead of us in line. They seem to have let go of their argument and are discussing what they want to see. Amy sees us and scowls in our direction. She turns away, and glaring at Brian as if it is his fault we are in line for a movie. We pay for our tickets, get our snacks and drinks, and start to head toward the theater to find seats. Amy is standing at the door waiting for us.

"Why are you following us? I don't appreciate you spying on us. We haven't done anything that would cause you to watch us all the time."

Brian must have gotten suspicious of how long she was gone. He walks out of the theater at the same time she starts asking us her questions. "Really Amy? You know how small this town is. It's not like there is a lot to do here. Just because they decided to have dinner and movie on the same night we did doesn't mean they are out to get us."

She narrows her eyes at us as she crosses her arms over her chest and juts her hip out.

I sigh. "He's right. We decided to have a date night and enjoy ourselves. We had no way of knowing what you were doing tonight. The only other option would have been to go play goofy golf, but since we are on a date and didn't want to make it a double date with Landon and Penelope, we went to the movie and they went to play goofy golf."

I can see in her eyes she really doesn't want to believe me. Chase and I find seats in the middle of the theater. Brian and Amy come a few minutes later. By the look on his face, he is pretty angry with her at this point. She walks to seats a few rows ahead of us, grabs their drinks, and goes to seats closer to the back of the theater. Brian stands there for a minute. He eventually picks up their snacks and goes to sits with her. Chase and I pretend to not notice any of this.

I decide that I'm not going to let them ruin our night. I have been looking forward to seeing this movie and a date with my awesome boyfriend. I watch him as he watches the previews for upcoming movies. With his dark brown hair and bright blue eyes that I lose myself in, I can't imagine feeling more in love with anyone else. Without looking over at me he leans over and whispers, "I brought you here so you can watch the movie you wanted to see, not so you can sit and stare at me all night."

I'm caught staring at him. He chuckles as my face turns pink. I whisper back, "The movie hasn't started yet." I then turn my attention to the screen.

After the movie is over, even though I really want to, I don't look over my shoulder at Brian and Amy. They were a few people behind us in the line to the door. I smile as I hear Brian comment, "See, they are just on a date. Not once did they look in our direction, or try to listen to what we were saying." I hear Amy sigh in frustration.

Chase looks over at me with a mischievous look in his eyes. "How did you like the movie? I thought it was ok, not really my thing though."

I wonder where he is going with this. I already know this isn't his choice for a movie. It was my turn to pick. "I loved it. It was everything I thought it was going to be."

He smiles. "Next time, I get to pick, so don't think you will be able to weasel your way out of seeing the next action movie that comes out."

Chase opens my door for me. When he gets in on his side, he is laughing. He sees my confused expression and lets me in on what he has been doing. "She was so convinced that we were trying to spy on them, I couldn't help but rub it in that they weren't even in our conversation. As I was talking to you, I could see her face. She was getting more confused by the second that our conversation was about movies and had nothing to do with them."

"Well, personally, I think our date had too much focus on another couple. I think you are going to have to work hard at making it up to me that I didn't get our nice date and night away from it all."

He grins at me. "Oh, believe me, I have ways to make it up to you." He winks at me and the butterflies in my stomach take flight.

CHAPTER 10

The next few weeks go pretty much the same. We have finals coming, so we spend extra time studying. Brian is still soaking up any information that he can about us and Amy is still watching suspiciously. We don't have a lot of time to worry about it.

We are still getting e-mails and phone messages from other people in the witch world that think that we are trying to take over. Getting the messages is hard, but there really isn't anything we can do about it. As long as they keep their distance and let us know about their position from afar, it really isn't hurting anybody. I am starting to get a little worried. The messages are not dwindling like they should be in my opinion. They stay the same. How long are they going to be content with just messages? How long before they get tired of sitting and waiting, and want something to actually happen? I can wait to discuss this with the others when we have more time to try and come up with a solution, but I'm still worried.

On the last day of school we are there for 15 minutes to

get our report cards, clear out our lockers. The tradition is, everyone meets at the beach after that and a start of summer party will last the whole day and into the night. Every student has their swim suits on under their shorts and tank tops so they are ready to go straight to the beach from the school. This year is no different.

We've been so stressed that I have been looking forward to this party. I am all smiles when we finally arrive. We have perfect weather, sunny with a slight breeze. Penelope and I lay out on a blanket to get a little sun before we get in the water.

Brian and Amy haven't made many friends. They've spent a lot of time with us, which Brian is using as a learning opportunity. Amy grudgingly goes along. They set their blanket along side of ours, and the guys start talking. We girls just enjoy the warmth of the sun soaking into our skin. It's nice to lay there and not have to worry anymore if I have studied enough.

After about a half an hour, we are hot and get in the water. Walking down the beach, I notice Amy is really distracted. I'm not sure how to ask without her being suspicious. Penelope has noticed too. We both try to watch her without her realizing what we are doing. The guys are lost in their conversation about different projects they want to do, and don't notice that anything is going on.

Finally, I can't take it anymore. "Is there something wrong, Amy?"

She shakes her head like she is trying to clear it, scowling at me as she crosses her arms over her chest. "Why would you think that something is wrong?"

"I didn't mean to pry. You seem distracted today. With finals being over, it made me think that maybe something else was going on you might want to talk about."

I can see the conflict in her eyes as she tries to decide if she trusts us enough to talk about whatever is bothering her. I don't want to push, so we wait patiently until she can make the decision for herself.

She sighs, the scowl leaves her face, and her arms drop to her sides. "I'm just confused about a few things. I know that you guys think I am a bitch, and really I am. I have never given you a chance. From the beginning I have had this notion of who you are, and I was not going to let you show me any other side of you. I was so ready to judge you before I had the whole story, I didn't realize I didn't have the whole story. Don't think this means I trust you, or I am just going to blindly believe anything that you tell me......it just means that I have accepted the fact that I might not know as much as I thought I did about you."

Penelope and I exchange a look. I am really glad that she is finally accepting that there is more to the situation than she knows. Penelope must feel the same way. "It's hard to change the way you view something you've been taught. We aren't going to ask you to change your beliefs. We're just glad you are willing to get to know us before you make any new judgments."

The guys have noticed something is going on. They have been listening to our conversation. Brian looks at Amy with pride in this eyes. She rolls hers back at him. We all laugh and let the matter drop. The rest of the day, we are able to hang out with other kids and just be normal teenagers again. I know now that school is out, the chance of other witches showing up increases, but I am trying not to dwell on that today.

Chase walks up behind me and wraps his arms around my waist. "I can't believe it. We are officially seniors now! Hopefully, our life doesn't get so hectic that we don't have time to talk about college. I don't think going to different schools will be an option. The four of us need to stay close to each other. We will have to sit down and discuss our options."

I have been giving this matter a lot of thought lately. It took me a while to come to terms with not proceeding how I had always planned. College was something that was going to come after high school and I saw it as a natural progression.

Now that our lives are so different, those plans had to be abandoned. I turn around in his arms and look up into his eyes, "I love that you want to talk about normal stuff like that, but we have to remember, we aren't normal. I don't think we'll be able to go away to college. We have to stay close to this area. The best we can do is go to a local college. With everything that goes along with who we are, I'm not so sure that's a good idea."

Chase frowns. "I see your point, but I think maybe we should discuss it with Landon and Penelope before we make any decisions about how we should proceed. I don't know if I'm ready to give up college, and I'm pretty sure that Penelope has never considered not going to college. I thought the three of us would take a year off until she was able to graduate high school, then the four of us would go together. Since we still have two years, we have plenty of time to discuss it and come up with a plan."

I smile and let the matter drop. He is right. We have two years before it will be possible, so there is no reason to dwell on it right now. Amy still seems preoccupied. As the sun starts to set, I notice that her anxiety level has not dropped. I am starting to wonder what is going on, but I know I won't get any other answer than what she gave us earlier. I had thought that was all it was, but since she is not acting like she is feeling any better about it, I am starting to think she only said that to placate us. Something else is going on. I don't think Brian knows anything about it, though because he isn't acting different than normal.

Penelope has noticed it too. I look over at her, she is watching Amy thoughtfully. When she notices that I'm looking at her with a question in my eyes, she just shrugs her shoulders and rejoins the conversation around us. Since there is nothing that I can do to make her tell me what is bothering her, I decide that we will have to deal with whatever comes our way. The party continues, and we get more relaxed. I find myself drug over to a group to clarify a story that two different people have different versions of. Chase loves all the stories. Some of the stories are great memories, but some of them are really embarrassing.

A couple of the guys on the football team start walking up behind Landon. They are trying to be really quiet, and putting their fingers over their mouths to let those of us that can see them know to not say anything. I act like I don't see them. When I can't hold in my laughter anymore, they are right behind Landon. We start laughing, clutching our sides, as the guys pick up a yelling and kicking Landon, and throw him out into the river.

When he surfaces we can see the grin on his face. This starts an all out war. Everybody is trying to throw somebody else in the water. I'm standing off to the side laughing at the way some of the girls are trying to bribe their way out of being thrown in. There are offers of dates, kisses, money, yard work, and anything else they can think of, to try and convince the guys not to throw them in. I'm particularly interested in the girl who took my spot on the cheer leading squad. She has gotten a few of the other girls to help her. They are sneaking up on her boyfriend who is searching for her. When the girls get to him, he is completely outnumbered by the girls, so there is really isn't much he can do to prevent it. They manage to get him to the water and push him in.

While I'm distracted, it doesn't occur to me to watch Chase to make sure he doesn't get any bright ideas. It is a mistake. Chase has positioned himself so the only thing he has to do is scoop me up and start running to the water. Since I can't use my magick against him, I really have no chance of not going in, but, if I am going in, so is he.

He doesn't pay attention to the fact that I am wrapping my arms around him tightly and locking my fingers together. When he gets about knee deep in the water and tries to throw me, I smile as he is pulled off balance and falls in with me. As soon as we hit, I let go and make my way to the surface. He comes up sputtering. I laugh as he looks at me with narrowed eyes, "You didn't expect me to go in without a fight did you?"

He laughs. "It did seem too easy. I wondered why you were trying to talk me out of it instead of trying to wiggle your way out of my arms. I have to admit that was a good one."

It takes a little while for it to calm back down. It is a long time before anyone trusts anyone else behind them. It's funny watching everyone trying to keep track of anyone who might throw them in the water. Finally, it looks like everyone has called a truce and a bonfire is started.

I don't know who brought them, but the ingredients for s'mores are passed around. It's nice to just sit on the beach. Since we have heard the same stories over and over again, it doesn't take long for people to start asking Chase, Penelope, Brian and Amy about things they have done in their other schools. Chase and Penelope tell stories about things people would do to the new kids at different schools. They try to keep the stories to ones that were just innocent fun, but some of them still show how cruel people can be.

Brian and Amy try to not get involved. Amy absolutely refuses to answer any questions. Brian is vague, and it looks like he might be making it up as he goes along. We can tell they are really uncomfortable. It doesn't take long before everyone quits asking. They do, however, take up a lot of Chase's evening. He is really good at telling stories. He makes you feel like you were there and a part of what was going on.

It starts to get late. The longer we sit there, the more distracted Amy seems to get. Brian is even starting to notice something is going on. She has been working hard all day to keep him from noticing, but now it's painfully obvious. As we head back to the blankets to start packing our stuff, he asks her about it. "What is going on? You are nervous about something, but I don't know what it could be."

She looks around at us before she turns pleading eyes on Brian, "Can we talk about this at home? I really don't want to get into it around all of these people."

Brian sighs in frustration. Whatever it is, she isn't going to reveal it in front of us. We figure it's something to do with us, but if Brian doesn't know about it, then it can't be anything we have to worry about right now. None of us are prepared for what happens next, not even Amy. My jaw drops to the ground when I hear a familiar voice. "I can't leave you guys alone for five minutes and you've already gotten yourselves into another mess."

Rayne is standing on the beach by our stuff with her hands on her hips and an amused look on her face. Next to her is one of the most perfect guys I have ever seen. He has black hair and grey eyes, his body is sculpted, and I can see his six pack abs, even from this distance. Chase and Landon roll their eyes at us as we check out the guy with Rayne. Amy looks stunned. Brian looks extremely pissed.

Rayne ignores the reactions to her appearance. She looks at Brian and Amy. "I'm Rayne Evans and this is Ethan Sanders, but I'm sure you already know that." She raises an eyebrow as she crosses her arms over her chest and juts her hip out. "Yes, I know who you are, and who you work for."

Brian tries to say something to Amy, but she has passed shocked and moved to pissed as well. Before he is able to begin saying what he wants to her, she gives Rayne a defiant look. "If you know that, then you should know why you were brought back to this piss ant little town in the middle of corn fields in Illinois."

As Rayne and Amy glare at each other, understanding blooms on Brian's face. "You told them that Rayne was needed to take care of things here, didn't you? I can't believe you. I thought we agreed it would take more time to assess the whole situation before we made any recommendations."

Amy looks guilty. "I did agree to that, but now that summer vacation is here they will have the time they need to start to put their plan into action. I can't let them get to the point where we can't stop them. They are just telling us what they want us to hear. They are manipulating us to try and make us think that they are the victims, and not the ones with the plot." She flings her arm in our direction.

Brian looks hurt. "I know that is what we have been told to believe. Don't you trust our instincts? We have talked about this."

Rayne has heard enough. "You two can have your dramatic fight later. I know why I was called here, and by whom. What you and everyone else don't understand, is I am *not* my father. I will not blindly follow orders and hurt people because I have been taught how. Yes, my father trained me to take over when he died. Yes, I have the skills. No, I have no desire to do any of that. I only came because these four can't seem to keep themselves out of trouble."

She looks at us. "As for you guys, you have really managed to get yourselves in a big mess this time. Do you realize the whole witch community is about two days away from storming this town to take care of you? You can't just ignore the problem and hope it goes away. The longer you ignore the messages you have been getting, the more convinced that they became that you were trying to do exactly what they thought you were."

We look at her in astonishment. It never crossed our minds. Rayne laughs. "You know, you four really need to come out of your own personal world and pay attention to what is going on around you more often."

Amy has gotten over her fear of Rayne. "You were called here to help clean up this mess. If you are not willing to do what you are supposed to, we will have to find someone who will. There is a long list of people that want the favor of the Council and will help us."

Rayne looks her up and down. "First, there is nobody better than me. Second, if you think you can get up in my face and tell me what I will or will not do, you are going to learn the hard way that I do things my way, and only my way. If you had taken your head out of the bag your parents have put it in, you would realize that you can't blindly believe anyone. You have to do your research and find out the facts by yourself."

Amy isn't used to being talked to in that manner. She is

used to being the one who is moody and bitchy and everyone else getting out of her way. I am interested to see which one of them is going to come out on top. Amy mutters "Bitch" under her breath.

Rayne smirks. "Yep, and I am damn proud of it. If you don't want to hear the truth, and you don't want to act like an adult and make your own decisions, then you need to go back to your nursery and let mommy tell you what to think and what to do."

She is done talking to Amy and turns back to us. "Ok, I know I can't go wherever it is that you guys go so you won't be overheard, so I have created another spot for that purpose. Meet me at this address in an hour." She hands me a piece of paper and starts to walk away. She gets about halfway to the parking lot when she calls over her shoulder. "It really is good to see you guys again, but you need to quit pissing people off so that I have to keep saving your asses." She smirks and walks the rest of the way to her car.

We exchange looks at each other and burst into laughter. Brian and Amy are completely lost. The looks on their faces prompt more laughter. Penelope finally feels sorry for them and starts to explain. She sighs and exaggerates the motions to cross her arms over her chest as she rolls her eyes at Rayne. "She may be a bitch, but she is one of the good guys. She helped us because it was the right thing to do. If you decide that you want to help, you are welcome to contact us. You have our numbers. We understand that you aren't going to want to stand up to the whole witch world, but we don't have a choice.

We aren't going to hold it against you if you decide to stay out of this fight. We hope you will realize that we aren't the bad guys, but that decision is up to you. If you stay out of it then no harm will come to you. But, if you fight with them, we aren't going to hold back because we know you." She turns her back on them and picks up her bag.

We finish packing up our stuff and head back to the car. Brian and Amy are still standing on the beach watching us when we leave the parking lot and head home to shower andf fill our parents in on what happened before we meet with Rayne and Ethan.

    I double-check the address to make sure we are at the right place. It is a huge house in the nicest part of town. When we knock, Rayne and Ethan open the door and gesture for us to come inside. We look around with amazement as Rayne shrugs her shoulders in nonchalance. "Ethan's dad is a surgeon and his mom is a financial adviser. They have plenty of money, but since my mom is a model and only stays home between jobs, she went in on the house so I wasn't left to my own devices. I really don't know what she meant by that." She winks at me to show that she is joking. She knows very well what her mom is worried about.

    I chuckle as she leads us toward the back. She stops halfway down a hallway and turns to us. I look around trying to figure out why we are talking in a hallway. She smirks and leans on the wall. I gasp as the wall opens. The door is well camouflaged. Now that I know, I can still barely see where it is.

    Before she walks into the room, she turns to us with a very serious expression. "As a precaution, you have to put your hand in the space of the doorway. The spell can then read your magick to determine if you have any intention of harm toward any of us. It's nothing personal, anyone who does not live here will have to do this each time they enter this room."

    I smile at her concern. "Don't worry, we're not offended. It's a good practice to have, especially right now when nobody knows who to trust. Ours is set up so nobody can enter except those of us that created the spell."

    She looks relieved and walks into the room with Ethan right behind her. We each put our hands up to the invisible barrier in the doorway and hold it there until it lets us pass through. Inside, we find plenty of chairs for us to sit down. There are three adults already in the room watching cautiously.

As we get settled, a woman who is an older version of Rayne starts the conversation. "I'm Renae Evans, and I want to thank you for releasing my Peter from what the Council did to him. It broke my heart to see what they did to such a good man and my baby girl. I owe you so much for releasing him and giving me back my daughter." She looks away and tries to wipe the tears that have formed in her eyes without us noticing.

We are stunned by her words. None of us know what to say. We had only been trying to save ourselves. We weren't prepared for her to thank us for killing her husband.

While she composes herself, Ethan's mom begins. "I'm Rose and this is my husband, Dale. We also want to thank you. Not being able to find his soul mate, Ethan has been miserable We moved in every lifetime trying to find her, but with no luck. After you finally broke the spell, and Rayne was open to find her true soul mate, it didn't take her long to find Ethan. We owe our son's happiness to you."

Ethan chuckles at our expressions. "We can understand that you don't feel like you've done anything to deserve the thanks that we are offering to you, but you do. Even though it was you at the center, none of what has happened was your fault. You were manipulated into the actions that best benefitted those pulling the strings."

Landon interrupts him. "How do you know?"

They exchange worried glances before Dale continues. "Rose and I were part of the group that was pulling the strings. I'd guess your parents have told you there were at least three families involved, and that wanted to take over the Council. We felt they had served their purpose and it was time for some younger leadership, at least that is what Rose and I believed. It turns out the other two families were the ones doing the manipulating.

We didn't realize what was happening until this lifetime. When we saw how you handled things this time around, I realized there must have been some magickal interference the other times before. Your actions were drastically different this time. It didn't take me long to fit the pieces together. They had been placing a spell on you when you were children, so you would fall into the same confusion every time it came time to make a decision about your soul mate. When Rayne and Ethan met for the first time, and it was apparent that they were soul mates, it came together for me.

I could finally see how they had manipulated everyone to bide their time until they were able to use you to take out the Council. They never let me in on the entire plan. They knew I would never sacrifice my son's happiness to gain power. I was the weak link. I wasn't in it to gain power, but to make it a better world for our people." He meets each of our eyes individually.

Rose takes her husband's hand and continues the story. "We aren't bad people. We are just like you, manipulated into doing what it was that best benefited the others. We always thought of them as family. It never occurred to us that they would betray us. When Rayne and Ethan found each other, there was no way to deny that we had been fooled."

Renae now has her emotions under control and jumps in. "I have watched as the Council destroyed my family and there was nothing I could do to stop it. I refuse to let anyone, the Council, or the other two families, destroy anyone else."

We exchange glances between us. I open the link between all of us. *"I don't think we should continue this tonight. We don't know if we can trust them. We should have our parents here for any discussions."*

Penelope interrupts. *"We don't have time to sit here staring at them before they figure out something is going on. Let's find a way to politely go and we can discuss this more at home with our parents."*

Landon responds before anymore time can pass. "It's nice to know that we have an inside point of view. I think our parents should be a part of any discussions about how we proceed from here. They have been helpful, and I think they can add some insight."

The adults nod. Dale speaks for the group. "I agree. I think they are very important to what we need to discuss. It is late. You kids head on home and get some rest." He stands and starts toward the door leading us out. Meet us here tomorrow about eleven, if that works, and bring your parents with you. We have much to discuss."

Back at the house, our parents are waiting up for us. We fill them in on what happened and let them know about the meeting the next day.

CHAPTER 11

I am still distracted by thoughts of last night's events the next morning. When we go downstairs, we find that our whole family is already there. We make our way to the secure room to talk before we leave for the meeting after a quiet breakfast. After we have found seats my dad starts. "How do you know that we can trust these people?"

I sigh. "We don't have anything to go on but our instincts. Mine are telling me that we should trust them. We are going to need their help."

My dad starts to say something else, but mom interrupts him. "Is it your instincts telling you this, or is the ancient magick guiding you?"

I look at the others who seem just as surprised as I am that none of us had thought about that. It doesn't happen often enough for us to depend on it, so we think of it as a gift when it happens. We take a minute to examine the feelings to determine where it is coming from. We nod to each other and I reply. "It is the ancient magick guiding us."

My mom lets out the breath she had been holding and

hangs her head. "Then, I guess we don't really have a choice do we? What worries me the most is the ancient magick only guides you when it is really important, which means their help is going to be a turning point. If we need that much help, this is going to get really bad."

She is right. If we are going to need that much help on top of our powerful magick, we are going to be facing some horrible things. I sigh. "We need to figure out how we are going to have them help us, without letting them know about the ancient magick. We agreed we shouldn't let anyone know about that."

Landon reminds us of a problem with the plan, "Rayne already knows about it. She told us about it, remember? As for the rest of them, everyone is looking in New England for the Origin. It has been believed for a long time that is where it all started. It should be easy to play it off as just another place of power. The ancient magick is only going to reveal itself to those it believes will be able to help us protect it. If they are not meant to know about it, they won't."

That makes sense. I see a problem though. "Rayne does know and I can't see her keeping that important bit of information from her soul mate, can you? She knew before us that the Origin was there."

Chase's mom looks at us with understanding on her face. "Maybe there is more to Rayne's part in this story then we originally thought."

We have to get going if we are going to make our meeting on time.

When we get there, Dale answers the door. He gestures for us to come in and follow him. The adults are looking around with awe. When we get to the hidden door, he looks nervous. "The only way for you to enter this room, is for you to place your hand in the doorway and let the protection spell read your magick. If you have no intent to harm anyone that lives here, the spell will let you pass through."

My dad looks at Dale with understanding. "That is not a problem. We expected some form of protection and a secure room."

Once everyone is in, introductions are made so everyone knows who everyone else is. Dale jumps right in. "I understand you have no reason to trust us, but I have some information that will be helpful for you. I was part of the group that has been studying you, and I can tell you what they know and how they plan to use it. I don't know their whole plan, but I have heard enough, and know them well enough, to have a pretty good idea of what they will do."

My dad has somehow become the spokesman. "We want to thank you for offering your help. We have a very good reason to believe you are really trying to help us and that we should trust you. Please forgive us for not disclosing our source, but it isn't up to us to reveal it."

The other group exchanges a look and Rayne nods her head. Dale indicates for her to let us in on what they knew. "I told them the Origin is here." She smirks with her arms crossed over her chest and her eyebrow cocked. "When I came back and wandered over there to do some thinking on how I wanted to reveal myself and my plan, I felt it. The ancient magick spoke to me. I know it is what is telling you to trust us and that you need our help."

She loses the smirk and her face turns serious. "What you don't know, is that Ethan and I are Guardians. I don't know the reasoning behind it picking all of us, but it has, and that has to mean something. I know you all have a bond and that you are very close, but that doesn't mean that you don't need friends too."

Chase is suddenly in all of our heads. *"I'm not sure about this. Why all of a sudden is she here claiming to be a Guardian? I think she might be trying to get information from us."*

I don't know to believe at this point. *"I know we have been blindsided, but what reason could she have for doing this?"*

Landon takes the lead. *"We can't sit here and argue about it. They are going to notice if we don't start saying something soon. Listen to your instincts and they will tell you that she is telling the truth."*

I turn to Rayne. "I'm glad we don't have to keep being a

Guardian a secret from you. It wasn't that we didn't want to tell you." I shift in my chair and push my hair behind my ear. "We didn't feel like it was our place. We believe if the ancient magick wants someone to know about it, it will reveal itself."

She smiles. "You didn't really think I wouldn't find out did you? Not much gets past me."

I laugh. "Wow, try not to be so down on yourself, you really should have some confidence."

We laugh at that, releasing the tension.

Dale makes a suggestion that has us stunned again quickly. "I know you are like family, and you have been a unit in every lifetime until this one. I am going to suggest that we all need to live closely now because what is coming is going to be hard to fight against. This house has plenty of room. I understand you might not trust us, but since the six kids are Guardians of the Origin, and we are here to support them in any way we can, it would be best if we had a central place."

We sit there stunned as Rose gives her husband a glare. "I'm sorry he dropped that on you like that. We discussed it last night and decided that it was a good idea. We were planning on talking to you about it today, but I thought it would be something we would lead up to. We will leave you here to discuss what you think about it, without us staring at you. Take as long as you need. Send Rayne a text when you are ready for us to come back in. As they are leaving we hear her start to lecture Dale on the way he handled that. "There were so many ways you could have brought that up, and you had to go with the least appealing?"

I chuckle at her scolding her husband. When they are gone I can see the conflict in the adult's eyes. I'm not sure what to think of the proposition. I want to hear what our parents think first. Mom starts tapping the heel of her shoe on the floor nervously. It is a habit I have only seen her do when she is trying to make a major decision. I suddenly feel small. "I don't know what to think. We meet these people today and they want us to abandon our homes to move in. I know with Rayne and Ethan being Guardians we need a central location, but why do we all need to live in this house?"

Landon's mom takes over. "I don't understand why this has to be done right now. Can we think about it for a while before we have to decide?" She uncharacteristically starts to fidget with her necklace. I have never seen her look nervous before.

Rachel interrupts. "I think you are both looking at this the wrong way. I understand your concerns, and share them, but there is more to consider. How can we expect the kids to have a close relationship with Rayne and Ethan if they are always apart? As much as we want to keep them safe, we will sometimes have to do things that we don't immediately feel comfortable with."

Mom huffs out a frustrated breath as she runs her hands through her hair. "I know we need to look at the big picture. If I take out my personal concerns, I have to admit it is a good idea. It would be great to not have to worry about the kids. If Rayne and Ethan are supposed to help them protect the Origin, it is important that they are close so they can create a bond and work better together. They would have more people helping to keep an eye on them too. We all need to learn different ways to do things, we have always done everything the same. We can help each other."

Now that mom has told us her opinion, she sits back and waits for someone else to give theirs. Landon's mom begins hesitantly. "I can see where you are coming from. I agree that it is a good idea, but I'm not sure what the consequences of this could be with five families under the same roof."

Landon lets out a groan as he looks at his mom. His frustration is written all over his face. "Mom, will you please look at the situation, not the consequences, and just make a decision for once. Sometimes, you just have to take a leap of faith and listen to your instincts."

She narrows her eyes at Landon and takes a breath. We all wait, not daring to move, for her reaction. She stands up and looks down at him. "You may be a Guardian of the Origin, and a very powerful witch, but you are still my son. I will not tolerate this kind of behavior. I have never allowed to you to talk to me like this before, and I am not going to start now. You may not want to look at what can happen, but someone needs to. I know I overanalyze everything, but have you ever stopped to ask me why? No, you sit there and complain about it. We are making decisions that affect a lot of people. I take that responsibility very seriously."

Landon's face loses color the more his mom chastises him. "I'm sorry. I didn't think about it that way. I know I shouldn't have talked to you like that. I am frustrated. I didn't mean to take it out on you."

I have to stifle a giggle as Chase opens the bond. *"Dude, nice save! I thought she was going to strangle you right there."*

Even in our heads we can hear the annoyance. *"Shut up. I have never seen her that pissed at me."*

Penelope clears her throat to cover the giggle trying to escape.

His mom sits down and addresses the entire room. "I agree, I believe it is a good idea. There is no way to weigh the outcomes, so I am fine with making the decision with the facts that we have."

Everyone in the room looks at her with slack jawed, shocked expressions. It is the first time any of us has seen her agree to take a leap of faith. Annoyed that we are shocked, she huffs. "Oh, come on! I am not that unreasonable. I like to make an informed decision, but since there is no way to do that in this situation, I don't have any choice but to do what I feel is right."

We laugh, then we look at Rachael. She is the only mom hasn't voiced her opinion yet. It seems like there is an unspoken consent from the men, this decision will be left up to the women. She sighs. "It would be nice to have both of my children living in the same house again. It is nerve racking not knowing where they will be sleeping or when I will see them. It is a good idea to have the extra help as well."

They look at us when she finishes. Since the adults have agreed it is a good idea, it is up to us now and what we think.

I know I feel like this is the right move, but I don't know what Chase, Landon or Penelope feel. Since Landon is the one that has a head for strategy, we let him lead.

"I can feel this is what the ancient magick wants us to do. I think it is bringing us together for a reason. We have to understand though, this is not temporary. If we agree, we have to fully commit, sell our houses, and completely move in here."

It is decided. We will be moving in to this huge house. I send Rayne a text. When they have settled into their chairs, we accept their offer.

Renae shares a few things that we did not realize. "I am not going to be here much after this whole mess is straightened out. My travel schedule is crazy. I will be here for a few weeks here and there, but not full time. Rayne will be here though. It is important to her not to have to travel around all the time. She said she already feels a bond with you four and could not leave with me. Also, there is plenty of room for everybody to have their own space here. That is the reason that we bought it."

For the rest of the afternoon the adults talk about moving details and mom selling the other houses. I am tempted to start leaving a trail of breadcrumbs as Ethan and Rayne show us around. It really is a huge house. I can easily get lost.

CHAPTER 12

We pack our belongings and move into the huge house. Renae was right, it is big enough for us to be comfortable and not feel like we are living on top of each other. It is nice. We are able to pick rooms that are not right next to our parents or each other. We will have privacy we have not had before.

Once we are settled, we meet in the secure room again. It is much quicker, since we can just walk in instead of having to stop and let the spell scan for ill intent. As soon as we are seated, Rayne begins in her usual straightforward manner. "Now that we have this situated, you four need to stop ignoring the problems, and start working on fixing them."

We are getting used to her mannerisms. It no longer offends us when she starts talking to us like this. It is just the way she is, she says what is on her mind, without the sugar coat, and no beating around the bush.

We look around at each other, not sure what she is talking about. She rolls her eyes and continues. "You have been getting e-mails, voicemails, and even some actual mail from other witches, saying they believe that you are trying to take over and they are not happy about it, right? By ignoring every attempt to get information, matters have gotten worse. Now they are almost positive you are the bad guys, because no denials or alternate scenarios have been presented, leaving them to assume you are guilty. You are going to have to work twice as hard to get redemption in their eyes. If you had stood up for yourselves from the beginning, it wouldn't have gotten this bad."

We hadn't thought about it like that. "Honestly, we figured if we didn't make any attempts to actually hurt anyone they would see we weren't like that. We weren't ignoring them, we didn't know what else to do. If we stood up and started getting angry, it would have proven their point. It seemed like a much better idea to just let it all blow over." I offer.

Rayne is looking at me like I have grown a second head, "And when things didn't get better, and the e-mails and voicemails kept coming, you never stopped to think that maybe your plan wasn't working? You never think past your immediate needs do you?"

I start to get angry but realize she is right. With embarrassment I reply. "Well, it's not like we did it on purpose. We didn't intentionally try to make it worse."

Ethan puts his hand on Rayne's arm. "Whether that was your intention or not, it is what happened."

Landon sighs, pinches the bridge of his nose between his thumb and index finger and he gives me a look. I smirk when I see Ethan give Rayne the same look. Chase huffs out a frustrated breath. They are going to have to step in between Rayne and I, and our verbal commentary often. The adults are flat out laughing. Dad calms down and puts a hand on my shoulder. "It is good for you to have someone that will challenge you. It will keep you on your toes."

I sit back pouting with my arms crossed over my chest, refusing to make eye contact with anyone. Dad turns to the rest of the group. "This should be interesting. Two strong personalities that don't think before they talk, in the same group and on the same side trying to work together. We won't be bored."

Rayne and I look at each other and shrug our shoulders. They are going to have to get used to it. Chase decides it is best to move on. "Is it really that bad? I don't see why everyone would get so worked up just because we broke free from a punishment and survived an assassination attempt."

Ethan quickly answers before Rayne has a chance to say anything. Judging by the look on her face, she knows he is doing it on purpose. It takes a great deal of effort on my part not to laugh, but I manage it. "It is not because you broke free and survived. It is they have been led to believe that you are out for revenge and power. The story is that when you broke free and you got your memories and full power back, you wanted to take revenge on the Council for placing the punishment on you in the first place, and now that you have power, you want more. In the eyes of everyone else in our world, you are pissed off, powerful teenagers, with no ability to think past the anger. They believe you don't care who gets hurt, as long as you can destroy the Council and take over."

As we look around, the adults not meeting our eyes and are fidgeting in their chairs, looking at everything but us. "You knew that is what they thought?! How could you not tell us what was going on, or that ignoring it was going to make it worse? How can the entire witching world hate us, and nobody mentioned it?" I am appalled and don't know how to react.

My dad holds up his hands in surrender. "Yes, we knew that is what they thought, but not that ignoring it would make it worse. We thought if we let them calm down, they would see that you haven't done anything to try to get to the Council. Only recently we heard that they believe you are just biding your time and working on your plan."

I shoot up out of my chair, start to pace, and run my hands through my hair. I am so frustrated that I can't sit still any longer. "And instead of talking to us about it, you let us continue to ignore it?"

He sighs. "We were trying to figure out what you could do to try to fix it. We hadn't come up with a plan yet, so there was no reason to worry you until we had a way to try to make it better."

I narrow my eyes at him. "For future reference, please remember we need all the information so we can decide what to do with it. We could have been working on a way to fix it ourselves. Just because you guys couldn't come up with any ideas, doesn't mean that we wouldn't."

He looks down at his hands and doesn't say anything else. Rayne takes advantage of the sudden quiet. She is looking at her nails on one hand and flips her hair over her shoulder with the other one as she interrupts haughtily. "Thankfully, you have us now, and we will be able to come up with a plan of action." We all roll her eyes at her.

She ignores our eye roll and continues. "First, we have to show that you are not power hungry or vengeful. The only thing they have seen as far as your personalities, is spoiled kids who do whatever they want. They don't know there was spell on you making you act the way that you were. They saw four teenagers, so spoiled and self-centered, they brought the wrath of the Council down on all of us. They blame you for the Council listening in, doling out punishments, and controlling them."

We are all shocked to hear that is what people actually think about us. Penelope lashes back. "None of that was our fault! The Council set this entire situation up. They used us as a tool to make sure everyone feared them and would do what they were told."

Ethan responds calmly. "We know that, but the only other people that do, will be working against you. Our biggest problem is all the other people, and what they have been made to believe. In close second, is the group that set this whole thing in motion, they were the Council's advisors. They were the ones who were down here and would report back to the Council who rarely left the Clouds. Their information was all the Council had to go on. Only when the Counsel started to keep a closer eye on everything themselves instead of just relying on their advisors, and saw that things were not as bad as they had been told, did they question the advisor's information.

The advisors had to find a way to stall so everything would be in place when they were ready. They were close, but it was going to be another couple of lifetimes before they had enough mistrust in the Council for them to be able to make their plan work. Since they were not able to find all of you so they could cast the spell that would keep the cycle going, it forced their hand early. They are doing their best to make the situation work for them, but since you have us, we will be able to stop them."

I have been trying not to react to Rayne's comments but there have been too many for me to be able to keep quiet any longer. "You know, we could have handled this ourselves if we had all the information. Instead of sitting there acting like we are idiots that would be lost without you, why don't you try to contribute something useful." I snarl.

Everyone in the room groans as Rayne's face turns red. Before she is able to respond Ethan jumps in. "I know we are under a lot of stress, but arguing with each other will only make it worse."

Landon has been listening intently through all of this. "Our strategy will have to be one that shows we are not trying to take over, but trying to protect them while at the same time exposing the advisors. Since you are helping us, it will help clear your name Dale, but you are still going to be a target for helping the advisors until now."

He nods his head. "I deserve whatever they want for me as a punishment. I may not have known the whole plan, and I may have thought I was acting on the belief I was helping everyone, but that does not excuse that I did not do any research or verify anything they were telling me. I simply went along with it because they had me believing it was for the best."

Penelope looks at him with sympathy and redirects the

conversation. "I don't think Amy will be any help. I am pretty sure she doesn't know the whole story. She is holding tightly to what she has always been told. Brian doesn't believe them anymore, he knows something is wrong with what he has been told, but he is not going to fight against his family, and definitely will not fight against Amy. We need to count him out as someone that can assist us. He might be able to get us some information, but I don't think he will be willing to."

Chase agrees. "I think he really wants to help but he can't to risk it. He has spent his lifetimes studying us and the information that he was being given was not adding up, but he had no way to verify if it was true or not. Now that he has finally had a chance to get to know us, and realizes that something else is going on, he can't do anything about it. It would come between him and Amy. I don't blame him. I wouldn't do anything that could come between me and Annisa either. He is an honest person and it would feel like a betrayal for him to feed us information, so I think that we shouldn't ask. We need to mark them off our list of possible allies."

Dale has a thoughtful look on his face. "I have gotten to know the people in that group well. Not as well as I thought I did, but well enough to know how they will go about doing things. You're right, the kids have never been given the whole story, and Brian has always thought something was off. His concerns were explained away by them telling him he just wanted to see the good in everyone even if it wasn't there. I never quite believed that, but I had no way to know for sure. Ethan you spent a lot of time with Brian and Amy, what do you think?"

"Brian is an honest person. He has a need to verify anything before he can just believe it. His mind works in such a way that he is able to look at the whole picture and see all of the possibilities. It comes in handy when he is working for you and figuring out the best way to go about something. The adults didn't want him to look at the whole picture though, just what they were feeding him. The curveball is Amy.

Amy is smart, but also manipulative. She can read people and know how best to play on their emotions to get what she wants. They encouraged her because it came in handy for when they wanted something that someone was not willing to give up. She could manipulate them into thinking it was a great idea. The only person that doesn't work on, is Brian. With his ability to see the whole picture and see all of the possibilities, he is able to see her manipulations for what they are. It is what makes them such a great team. It also makes it hard for her to keep anything from him. I am surprised she was able to keep him from finding out that Rayne had been called in."

I think about that for a minute. "He knew something was going on. I think she was worried about what his reaction was going to be. She was distracted and distant the whole day. Brian kept watching her, but he hadn't figured it out until you two showed up on the beach. He didn't seem surprised that you were there, just that he hadn't figured it out before that. I was surprised she still felt the way she did about us. She had done a pretty good job of pretending she believed there was more to the story. I think Brian may have been overconfident in his ability to see her manipulations. She got the information on us that they wanted, and kept Brian from knowing she was not trying to get to know us to form her own opinion, but so that she could use the information against us."

Rayne snorts at this. "Man, you really have to accept the fact that not everyone is going to like you and you can't help everyone. It is what gets you in the most trouble."

I narrow my eyes at her. I don't care that she is right, I am not ready to admit that out loud yet. "So, what I am supposed to do? Hate everyone and not give them a chance? I think you have that covered for all of us Rayne."

Chase interrupts before the argument can escalate any further. "We really need to concentrate on how the people are going to come at us, and what the advisors are going to do to encourage them. I really don't understand their plan.

How does having the whole witch world against us help them in trying to force our hand into destroying the Council so that they can take over?"

Landon has an answer. "That's easy. If the people come after us, and threaten to expose magick to the rest of the world, the Council will have to step in to keep it out of the public eye. When they are here, they will attempt to finish what Peter started, and make it look like it was just a casualty of the situation. Since we are more powerful, the advisors are assuming that when we try to protect ourselves, we will destroy the Council because they will not back down until they are successful. The advisors are telling the Council that they can destroy us, and they are seeing us as teenagers and not that big of a threat. They are confident in their belief that they are more powerful and will win."

Penelope summarizes. "We just have to find a way to show the people we are not the threat before they start to come here to destroy us. The Advisors are going to see what we are doing and work against us and try to make everyone believe that we are lying of course. So we have to be more convincing than they are."

We watch her and wait for her to continue. When she doesn't I finally ask, "And how exactly, are we supposed to do that?"

She shrugs her shoulders, "I have no idea. That is what we have to figure out."

CHAPTER 13

I am getting better at finding my way around the house. A trip to the bathroom no longer takes an hour as I try to find it, but is down to 15 minutes with only one or two wrong turns. You would think in a house this big with so many bathrooms it wouldn't be so hard to find one. You would be wrong.

The thing I like best is the in-ground pool in the back yard. There are hired companies that come in to take care of the yard, the pool, the cleaning in the house, and the maintenance for the house. It is great to be able to focus on what we need to be working on without our mothers constantly giving us some chore for household cleaning or maintenance. The best part of my day is laying in the pool on floats, throwing around different ideas on how to get out of our current mess. Today while floating, letting the sun brown our skin, Rayne gives one of her signature responses to a suggestion that had been made. "Sure, we can do that, and then just stand there and let them rip you apart."

I sigh and turn my head so I can look at her, "You know, your smart-ass comments really aren't helping."

She smirks. "I disagree. They make me feel much better."

I splash water at her as I direct my float to the other side of the pool. I don't know why I even try. Nothing will ever get her to stop making her comments. Penelope continues like our little side conversation never happened. "We need to think bigger. Everything we have come up with is for problems on a smaller scale. Most of the suggestions would work if it were only a few people. The problem is we are not thinking of things that will work on a large scale. We need something that can be seen by everyone, not just whoever happens to be there at the time."

Landon is surprised, "I don't know why I hadn't thought about that before. We need something that once we do it, no matter how much the Advisers try to keep it quiet, everyone will talk about and everyone will hear about it."

Chase adds his opinion. "It will have to be more than one thing though. If we just do one big thing, they will think we are just trying to put a good face out there. We need a series of things they can see so that it shows them we are trying to help not harm. The biggest problem is, we have to do them from here. We can't leave the Origin unprotected, and we can't leave it with just two Guardians."

Limiting the location makes it complicated. If we had the option to travel to different areas to explain ourselves and help, it would be much simpler. This pattern continues for longer than we would like as we try to figure out what we can possibly do from here that the Advisors will not be able to twist for their own benefit. None of us are coming up with anything that would have the impact that we need.

I am completely discouraged. "We are never going to think of anything. There is nothing we can do from here that they aren't going to twist to their own version. And, even if we did, how exactly are we going to get word out so that anyone hears about it?"

Rayne seems to have an endless supply of snarky

comments. "That's a great idea. Let's just give up and wait to see what happens. We shouldn't try to fix anything. If they want to believe we are going to try and destroy them, that's their problem, right?"

I ignore her. I am surprised when Chase agrees with her though. "She's right. Baby, we can't give up. Just because we haven't thought about it yet doesn't mean that it's impossible."

I am discouraged and feeling defeated so I am not in the mood to be lectured, and I am unreasonably angry about him agreeing with Rayne. I get out of the pool. "I'm going to take a shower."

When I come out of the bathroom wrapped in a towel, Chase is sitting on the bed. I narrow my eyes at him. "You are going to get the bed soaked sitting on it in wet swim trunks." Apparently I am not over being mad at him. He looks down at his shorts, which is when I notice that he has changed into regular shorts and is not wearing his swim trunks anymore. I am still mad, so instead of apologizing I walk over to my dresser and start getting out a pair of underwear and a bra so I can get dressed. I can feel his eyes boring a hole in the back of my head. I am still pretty mad. I snap, "What!?"

He is getting angry too. "You may be feeling defeated, but that is no reason to take it out on me. I do know that I don't deserve it."

As I spin around, all the anger surges to the front. "You side with Rayne and you lecture me on how I should feel, and you don't know why I am mad at you? We are supposed to be a team, and you sat down there and talked to me like I was a child who was throwing a temper tantrum. I was feeling discouraged and instead of trying to cheer me up, you treated me like I had no reason to feel that way. I expect that kind of thing from Rayne, but not from you."

His jaw dropped when I started yelling at him. By the time I am done, I can see his anger matches my own. "I was trying to help you see that there was still hope. If you don't want me to try and help, maybe I should just stick with sitting here looking good but not say anything at all." With that he gets up off the bed and walks out of the room, slamming the door on his way.

I sit down and the tears start flowing. I know it is not his fault, and I really have no idea why I got so mad at him. It isn't like he was attacking me or anything. Cried out, I get dressed. My hair is a mess since it dried before I brushed it. I do my best trying to calm it, finally give up, and put it in a messy bun. I am not sure what I should do now. I feel bad about the way I treated Chase. He was right. He had been trying to help. I want to go and find him, but I also want to give him time to calm down. My anger at him may have been unwarranted, but I deserve every bit of anger he is feeling towards me right now.

When I concentrate on his emotions I can feel that he isn't mad at me anymore, but I am confused by what I am sensing. Why would he be feeling content when we had just had a fight? I am depressed and embarrassed, but he is feeling happy. I can't take not knowing, so I go looking for him.

When I find him, I stand in the doorway for a minute. He and Rayne are sitting in the library deep in conversation. I can't hear what they are saying over the pounding of my heart. I can still feel his emotions are content, and he seems to be feeling more excited. I must have made a sound as both of their heads snap up at the same time. As soon as I see their faces, I break free from the trance I seemed to be in, turn, and run from the room.

I have barely gotten down the hall when I can hear them both following me. Chase keeps calling out my name. I ignore him and keep running, out of the house, and into the small area of woods adjacent to the back of the property. I run until I am at the lake that sits back in the woods. It is a very peaceful place and I come here often to think. I am seeking out the comfort of this place while my mind tries to come to terms with what I had seen.

It feels like my heart has been ripped out of my chest and

torn to pieces before it was shoved forcefully back into me. I don't know what to think. The connection I feel with Chase is supposed to mean that we are soul mates. Rayne found her soul mate when she met Ethan. How can this be happening? I hear Chase and Rayne behind me, but I don't turn around to face them. I stare out across the small lake, watching the water ripple as fish come up to the surface to eat the bugs that are resting there.

When they realize I am not going to acknowledge their presence, Rayne has no patience left. "You know, you really are a drama queen. If you had stopped to listen to what was actually going on, we could have all avoided this run through the woods. Did you even hear what we were talking about, or did you just see us sitting there, in opposite chairs, across from each other talking, and completely overreact?"

I spin around to face them. "I felt bad for the way I overreacted in the pool. I caught Chase's emotions so I could tell if he was calmed down enough for me to find him and apologize, and all I felt was that he was happy and content. So when I walked in and you two were so cozy, sitting there talking and enjoying yourselves, and he was all happy and content, I couldn't hear anything except my breaking heart." I cross my arms over my chest and glare at them both. Chase looks like he is afraid to move and talking is not something he is going to chance at the moment.

Rayne however, just rolls her eyes at me. "If you had taken the time to actually try and figure out what was going on before you ran off like a two year old, you would have heard what we were talking about and found out that is what he is so happy about. Not that he was talking to me, but what he was talking about." She spins on her heel and walks away.

I stare at where she had been standing, no longer sure what is going on. I look over at Chase. He is not mad about how I reacted, but he is still waiting until he can feel in my emotions that it is safe for him to talk. After a few minutes, when I finally realize I had completely overreacted before I knew what was going on, he starts to say something.

I put my hand up to stop him before he gets started. "I want to say something first. I'm sorry I was so unfair to you earlier. I was discouraged. I am really getting stressed that we can't find a way to fix this, but that isn't your fault. It was wrong for me to take my frustrations out on you. I know you were trying to help and I wouldn't let you. I also know that you and Rayne were just sitting there talking."

He tries to say something but I continue before he can say anything. "I'm not done yet. We just had a huge fight and you had just walked away from me again. You didn't come back and try to work things out, you stayed away. Then I could feel how happy and content you were, and that you were starting to get excited and I saw you with Rayne. I got jealous. I hated that I was miserable because we were fighting, and you were enjoying yourself."

He waits a minute. "Is it my turn now?" I nod.

"I forgave you for the way you reacted in the pool and after your shower before I made it down the hallway. I know you are stressed. All of us are feeling discouraged. Each of us is on edge, and small fights like this are going to happen. When I got downstairs, my mom found me and gave me something that she had been looking for since we moved in here. I had asked her about it, but she couldn't remember where she had packed it. She finally found it and that is what I was talking to Rayne about."

I look at him completely confused. He had not said anything to me about asking for something from his mom. I can't even come up with anything that she would have that he wanted that badly. He walks up to me and grabs my hands. He looks in my eyes and I can see all the love he feels for me pouring out of him. He then gets down on one knee.

"I was going to plan this elaborate night to do this, but I think this is perfect. Annisa Lawson, I love you with every fiber of my being. I am not complete without you. You make me the happiest man alive. I want the world to know that you are mine. Will you marry me?"

He pulls out a beautiful ring from his pocket. For the first time in my life I am speechless.

CHAPTER 14

"I bought this ring for you many lifetimes ago. It has always been put in a secure spot, and I showed my mom where it was so we would be able to get it when we got our memories back in each lifetime. This is the first time that I am actually able to give it to you. In the past, the memory of this ring would not come until I accepted that our fates would not change. This time, it did not present itself until I was ready to give it to you. I am really glad you weren't able to hear what I was saying to Rayne, so I could do this right."

His eyes haven't left mine since he started his proposal. I have tears streaming down my face, but I refuse to look away. After a minute he stands up with fear in his eyes. "Baby, you kinda have to say something here. If you're not ready to take this step, I understand."

I look at him confused for a second and then realize that I haven't answered him. I smile the biggest smile I have ever smiled, reach over and pulled him to me and our lips crash together. When we come up for air he smiles. "So, is that a yes?"

I laugh. "Of course, I will marry you. Did you really have any doubt as to what my answer would be? I had no idea you were thinking about proposing."

He grins. "That was the whole idea. You weren't supposed to know. I wanted to plan this elaborate date and give you the proposal people would be talking about for years, but it felt right doing it here, just us."

"I agree. I don't need everyone to talk about it, I just need you." Pulling me close, he kisses me with more passion than usual.

I admire my ring as we head back to the house. It is beautiful, and exactly what I would have picked out. When we get closer, I start to get nervous. Before we walk out of the woods I stop. Chase looks back to see why I stopped, and he puts his finger under my chin to look at him when he sees the panic in my eyes. "What is it? What's wrong?"

It takes me a minute to get the words out. "We have to tell our parents that you are seventeen and I am sixteen, and we are engaged."

He laughs. "That's what you're worried about?"

I nod my head. I am suddenly having a panic attack about what my parents are going to say about this new development. As the panic gets worse, Chase hugs me, holding me against his chest. "Baby, calm down, I promise everything will be fine. I asked your dad's permission, and I talked to my parents before I had my mom look for the ring."

I let out the breath that I hadn't realized I have been holding as relief floods through me. "I don't know why I was so panicked. I just kept seeing my parents being mad and forbidding us to get married."

He laughs. "You have to give your parents more credit than that. They were actually excited about it. Of course, they thought it was going to be a little bit later after I had time to plan it all out, but I don't think that will matter."

I feel much better as we walk back up to the house. My very angry father is standing inside the front door waiting for us with his arms crossed over his chest. He immediately looks down at my hand and sees my ring. I stop dead in my tracks at the look on his face. I look up at Chase and see he is just as scared as I am about how my dad is acting. "Both of you follow me, now."

He turns and starts walking down the hall. We don't have any other option except to run, but that isn't a real option so we follow him. He looks over his shoulder to make sure that we are following him. He stops in front of a room that I have never been in before. He looks at us. "We really need to talk." With that he opens the door and walks in.

I look at Chase and see my fear reflected in his eyes. We each take a deep breath and walk into the room to face my dad. As soon as we enter, we stop and stare around at the room with our jaws hanging open. We are in a ballroom. I didn't think houses had ballrooms anymore, but here it is. The room is filled with people.

There are a few people I recognize, and some I can tell that I have met in past lifetimes, but I don't have those memories yet. Everyone yells 'Surprise'. I study Chase's face. He is just as astonished as I am. My dad returns to us laughing, "You should have seen the looks on your faces! You would have thought I was leading you to the gallows." He pulls me into a hug and whispers in my ear. "I love you very much and I am so very proud of you. You will have a happy life and a really good marriage." When he pulls back, I can see the tears in his eyes that he is trying to hide. I have no hope of hiding mine. They are streaming down my face.

He pulls Chase into a hug next. I can hear what he whispers into Chase's ear. "I am proud to have you marry my daughter. I know I can trust you to take care of her, respect her, and keep her out of the trouble she always finds herself in." When he pulls back this time, both of them are trying to hide the tears. When my dad walks away, the others in our group come up one by one to congratulate us and tell us how happy they are for us.

Rayne has purposefully stood back and let the rest of

them congratulate us first so that she can be the last one. When she walks up, she gives Chase a hug first. "I'm so happy that things have finally worked out the way they are supposed to." She then hugs me. When she pulls back she has a serious expression on her face. "You get to make it all about you now, Drama Queen, but just for this afternoon." She smirks at me and walks over to Ethan. I laugh, glad that everything is back to normal with her.

My mom walks up to us when she sees me looking around at all the people here. "We knew Chase wouldn't be able to wait once he had the ring in his hand. Rachael pretended she had to find it so we would have the extra time we needed to throw this party together. One of the first things you can do to show the people around you that you are not trying to destroy them, is to invite them to celebrate something with you. If you were the power hungry dictators they thought you were, then you would make them attend your wedding or something like that, not send them an invitation and give them the chance to say no to your engagement party."

We have been racking our brains for a week trying to find a way to get the ball rolling on proving our intentions, and our parents have been working on their plan the whole time. She can see that I am frustrated they didn't tell us.

"We couldn't tell you. We didn't want you to get engaged to try and fix a mess. We wanted you to do what you felt was right and what you wanted. We knew you would say yes, but we wanted to make sure you were confident in your decision and that you knew you had made it for yourself, not an agenda."

I understand. I am glad they gave this to us. I was able to decide for myself, and after learning about how I had been manipulated in every life time before this, that was really important to me. I feel like things are finally starting to go the way they were always meant to. I nod to let her know I understand. She smiles and pushes us out toward all the people. "Now, go mingle and have fun."

We walk around and try to talk to everyone here, thanking them for coming to celebrate with us. A woman asks how long the engagement will be, and how soon we plan to get married. We haven't had a chance to talk about any of that, but Chase looks at me the first time we are asked, leaving that up to me. I look up at him with a question on my face. He smiles.

"I want you to have the wedding you have always dreamed of. Whatever time of the year, and however long you want to wait, is fine with me. I would marry you today if that is what you want."

I laugh. "I don't think I can plan a whole wedding in one afternoon." I look over at the woman who asked and see the amusement on her face. "It will probably be a year. I want a summer wedding, and I think we should probably graduate high school first. Next summer will give me plenty of time to plan."

Now that we have a time frame, it is a lot less uncomfortable as we are talking to people. We don't want to look like we have planned this just to get them here, so it helps that we can give them a time frame and the reasoning behind picking that time. As we are walking around talking, I notice Brian and Amy standing off in a corner. Brian looks miserable, and Amy looks livid. I'm sure their parents are here too, but we haven't met them yet. I'm not sure what is going on with them, but I don't think it could be anything good. I look up at Chase, nudge him to get his attention, and tip my head in their direction so he will notice them as well. He looks where I am indicating and watches them for about a minute.

He turns away and looks at me. "Today is about us and our lives together. We can deal with whatever they have planned tomorrow." He leans down and gives me a sweet kiss.

I agree. I don't want to deal with Amy or any of her drama today, so I push it from my mind and enjoy talking to others. Some of the people look genuinely happy for us while others look suspicious. I decide that there is nothing we can do to change their opinions, except be ourselves and let them see for themselves what kind of people we are.

I am so involved talking to everyone, and enjoying all the congratulations, that I have completely forgotten about Brian and Amy. Then, we walk up to a group of four adults. As soon as they introduce themselves, Chase and I both tense and wait to see what they are going to say or do.

One of the men greets us. "Hi, I'm Danny Williams, this is my wife Claire, and our friends Greg and Chloe Leeman."

We have finally met Brian and Amy's parents. I instantly look over to the corner where I last saw Brian and Amy. Brian looks nervous. Amy has a smirk on her face. Chase looked over at them as soon as I had. I can tell he doesn't like the look on Amy's face any more than I do.

Danny sees where we are looking. "I know you have already met my daughter Amy, and her soul mate Brian. They are good kids. Thank you for taking them under your wing, showing them around the school, and being so gracious to them when we moved here."

He is the salesman. He has that slimy charm that is so often there with the salesmen that are trying to sell you a car that is worth $1,000.00 for $10,000.00. I know not all car salesmen are like that, but I can tell that he is. I notice Chase is trying to wipe his hand on his pants so nobody can see what he is doing. I don't blame him. I am just glad that he only wants to shake Chase's hand, and I don't have to touch him. We are polite and talk to them for a few minutes, then make an excuse about still needing to thank so many people for coming to celebrate with us. Amy finally emerges from the corner when we walk away from them. Brian is following her, but he does not look happy about it.

We stop and wait for her to catch up to us. There really is no reason to avoid her. She is going to say what she wants and make the scene that she wants regardless of how long it takes her. The others in our group have apparently been watching Brian and Amy as well. As soon as they start making their way over to us, so do Landon, Penelope, Rayne, and Ethan. Our parents are mixed in the crowd keeping an eye on what is transpiring, prepared to step in if we need them.

I very slightly tilt my head in the direction of Brian and Amy's parents. My dad takes the hint, looks over at them, and realizes that he doesn't recognize them. He looks over to Dale. Dale gives an almost imperceptible nod to my dad. Now that I know the adults will keep an eye on the Leemans and the Williams', I can focus on Brian and Amy and whatever she has planned.

Amy still looks visibly angry when she walks up. I think she was counting on us being intimidated by her parents. She isn't happy that didn't happen. When they reach us, the rest of our group has gathered behind us. Amy puts her hands on her hips. "Do you really think you are fooling anyone? We know this is just an elaborate plan to try and get people to trust you so that you can take over."

I expect my anger to flare up at her words but I am strangely calm. I simply respond. "I'm sorry you feel that way. I don't know what I have done to make you not trust me, but I am sorry for whatever it was. Please feel free to enjoy the food and the party."

I turn my back on her and look at Penelope. I can feel Amy is preparing to throw a spell at me. She is even angrier that she isn't able to get me to react to her in anger and make myself look worse. I make sure to make eye contact with each of my group and shake my head no. I want to make sure they know I feel it, and I don't want them to do anything to stop it. Chase gives me a look like he can't believe what I am trying to tell him. I let the determination show in my eyes, and I see the acceptance in his. All of this happens in a matter of seconds. As Amy's spell hits me in the back, I fall to the ground. The room around me explodes into chaos.

CHAPTER 15

I know what I am doing is a gamble. I also know that this is the big event we need, to show people how we are and that we aren't trying to destroy them. My group forms a circle around me on their knees, making sure I am alright. She had thrown a very weak spell. It was only supposed to make me do something to her to make it look like I had attacked her. I reassure them I am fine and stand up.

I look around the room, stunned by what I see. The people that had been on the fence about us have made their decision. The Leemans and Williams' are losing their smirks as they slowly realize that Amy had been the one to show her vindictiveness, and we haven't done anything to make ourselves look bad. Her throwing a spell while my back was turned is considered the most cowardice act of a witch. The fact that they could feel a small amount of magick had been used, also proved that she had only done it to get a reaction. Everyone is now glaring at Amy, Brian, who is trying to hide his face in shame, and their parents.

A look of panic crosses Amy's face when some in the crowd start insisting on the arrest for her crime. She turns her pleading eyes to her father. Danny walks over and looks out at the crowd. "Let's not overreact. She is a teenager who has a hard time controlling her temper. Annisa here tried to steal her soul mate Brian away from her. Amy just didn't handle it very well."

Everyone in our group is staring at him with our jaws resting on our chests at his lie. Brian is even looking at him as if he can't believe what the man has spoken. Then we hear from the crowd, "Oh, come on. You don't really expect us to believe that do you?"

Danny's salesman face doesn't even flinch as he continues. "We have seen how she behaves. She thinks she can just have any boy that she wants. She doesn't have the same respect for soul mates the rest of us do."

A woman we had talked to earlier, who had clearly been on the fence about trusting us, stepped forward with anger written all over her face. "If that were true, then the two of them would not have gotten engaged. Yes, we have watched many times as the four of them repeated the same mistakes, which was suspicious in itself by the way, but we also saw that none of them ever married because they didn't have the trust needed for it. So, if there was truth in anything you are trying to make us believe, then they wouldn't be engaged."

Danny only falters for a moment, "You saw how shocked he was when I told you what happened. None of them knew what she had been up to. Amy happened to walk in on Annisa trying to seduce Brian."

When he started, Chase had wrapped his arm around my waist and pulled me close to him. He still has a good grip around my waist and is pulling me tighter against him. Everybody happens to look over at us when Danny says this last part. Just the way that we are standing discredits his statement.

To the surprise of everyone in the room, Brian steps around Amy with a very angry look on his face. He jabs his finger in my direction. "I have had enough! Annisa has never been anything but a friend to me. She never attempted to seduce me. She never even flirted with me. She is completely in love with Chase." He flings his arm in Chase's direction.

Turning to Amy, he points directly at their parents. "I love you. I can't imagine my life without you, but you are letting them change you. I can't take the lies, the schemes, or the manipulations anymore. You have a choice. You can choose to come with me and walk away from it all, because that is what I am doing right now, or you can stay and help them in whatever it is they are planning." His face is bright red with anger. He clenches his fists trying to stop the trembling in his hands.

Amy looks at him in shock. It is obvious she never expected him to give her an ultimatum. She looks between her father and Brian. After a few minutes of waiting, Brian lets out a defeated sigh, his shoulders cave, and his head drops. "I'm sorry, but I can't stay. If you ever change your mind and decide to leave this craziness, you know how to find me."

Amy turns to me, furious as she points at me. "You will pay for this. I will not let you get away with causing me to lose my soul mate." She looks at her father with a look of complete devastation.

Danny looks around, sees the hostility from everyone in the room directed toward him, and gestures for the others in his group to follow him. He walks up to Amy who is now sobbing, grabs her arm and drags her from the room. As he passes us he says low enough that only we can hear, "This isn't over. You may have won this battle, but the war is far from over, and we will win in the end."

They leave without looking back. I look at the others in my group. They have the same worried look on their faces that I can feel on mine.

It doesn't take long for people to start coming up to us, saying how they think Amy should be arrested for her unprovoked attack and made to answer for her actions. I reply it is something that doesn't need to be done. She is a teenager following the example that she was given on how to do things. It really isn't her fault she was taught to act like that.

The more people hear me say that, the more respect I can see in their eyes. I feel terrible for what happened between Brian and Amy, I would never want to break up soul mates. I can't imagine how painful it would be if Chase left me, but there is nothing I can do to change what happened. I decide I am not going to let Amy and the advisors ruin my night. This is a party to celebrate my engagement to Chase. I am not going to let it be overshadowed by a few unhappy people. Chase and I start mingling again. A catered dinner is brought in. And afterwards a band comes in and sets up. We dance until late.

When we are heading back to our room Chase asks, "Aside from the crazy Advisors, did you have fun tonight?"

I smile up at him. "Nothing could have ruined tonight for me. I was celebrating being engaged to the most handsome, kind, giving, and loving man on the planet. The fact that I got to tell so many people that you were mine, and how happy I am, was the best way to spend my evening. The Advisors were just a small discomfort that was well worth the rest of it."

"I have to agree. I hate that they had to put a stain on our celebration, but I'm glad you were able to see past it and enjoy the party. I don't know how I am going to wait a whole year to be able to call you my wife. The fact that you are wearing that ring to show everyone that you are taken will help though." He winks to let me know he is joking.

I elbow him in the side. We make it back to our room and have our own private celebration before we fall into an exhausted sleep.

At breakfast, my mom looks at me with worry in her eyes. "I'm sorry you had to deal with all of that when we were celebrating your engagement. I shouldn't have invited them."

I hug her. "It's not your fault they are miserable and try to bring everyone down with them. It was a small bump in the road that didn't cause any damage."

She frowns. "The party was supposed to be a special night to celebrate your engagement and they had to make a scene."

I smile. "Mom, really I'm fine. It sucked that it happened at our party, but it was something that needed to be done. I let it go and didn't let it ruin our night."

She lets out a relieved breath. "I'm so glad that you still enjoyed yourself. I was worried that you would stress about it, get all worked up, and not have fun."

I laugh. "It was a beautiful party and I had so much fun. Don't worry so much."

Rayne has been quiet through all of this, which is unusual for her. I am about to ask her if something is wrong when she smirks at me. "So, your reputation precedes you, and you still come out smelling like roses?"

Ethan shoots orange juice out of his nose and Penelope chokes on the milk she has just taken a drink of. While Ethan is trying to get the stinging to stop and Landon is pounding on Penelope's back to get her breathing regularly again, we laugh until our stomachs hurt. Chase looks over at Rayne. "Thanks, we needed that."

Ethan and Penelope both frown at him. Ethan counters, "I really don't think I needed orange juice to come out of my nose. That really hurts."

That has us laughing again When Rayne is able to calm down enough to talk she continues. "I try. You know you would all be boring sticks in the mud if I wasn't here to liven things up a bit."

My mom shakes her head at us and changes the subject. "Well, the Advisors actually did us a pretty big favor with that little show last night. They showed their true colors. Now that all of those people were able to catch Danny trying to manipulate his way out of the hot seat, but it will spread like wild fire. Our world could teach the high schools a little something about how to circulate a story quickly. I wouldn't be surprised to hear that the 30 messages on the voicemail are witches from all over the world apologizing for their behavior and offering their assistance if we should need it."

I am stunned. "Do you really think that is all we will need to do for our redemption?"

My dad snorts, which is weird because I have never heard him do that before. "Not even close. This is just the beginning. I know you are anxious to have people see you in the light you deserve, but it is going to take time. It took lifetimes for them to come to the conclusions they have. It is a good start, so they will start looking at you with an open mind, but you are far from redemption."

I lean back in my chair and pout. Chase chuckles, "Baby, redemption is not something instantaneous. You have to work for it. It took a long time to get to where we are, and now we have to work to get out of it."

I look over at him, still pouting. "It's not our fault we were acting the way we were. We were under a spell. How is it fair that now that we are no longer under the spell that we have to work so hard to convince everyone else that we are not bad people? It was someone else that caused this whole mess. Why are we stuck cleaning it up?"

Rayne smirks. "The witching world is not some magickal fantasy land where everyone walks around laughing, smiling and talking in the third person to make sure there are no misunderstandings. Get over it."

Even I can't help but join in the laughter at that comment. Rayne has successfully relieved the tension about the whole situation. We spend the rest of breakfast with our parents giving us background information on some the people we met yesterday. Bored, I am having a hard time keeping backgrounds straight.

My dad notices our eyes are starting to glaze over. "This really will come in handy. If you learn some things about the people you will come into contact with, they will notice. They will appreciate that you took the time to get to know about them. Everybody likes to be recognized and remembered. If you are constantly telling people, I'm sorry but I don't remember you, they are going to remember that too. You want to give the impression that you care about them. If you act like you can't be bothered to learn about anyone in your world, it will just strengthen the Advisor's position. People will start to think that your charming personalities at the party were just for show. If you want to keep the momentum rolling, you have to give it a little push in the right direction."

What he is saying makes sense, so we sit up and pay attention. We spend a few hours learning stories about people from the dads. After each story, the moms explain who each of the people are. The women describe the clothes of each person which helps us to know who the story is about.

After a few hours we have learned about as much as we can about who had been at the party last night. Dale stands up. "Ok, let's all go out by the pool."

We stand up confused but we follow him. Apparently, the adults have a plan because they group up facing us on the edge of the pool. We look at them, waiting for an explanation. Chase and Penelope's mom, Rachael, is excited when she announces, "We are going to start training you in some different types of magick. We each have our own styles and it will be good for us to learn from each other. Our group has always done things a certain way, and so has their group. Now that we have joined, we need to combine them and find the way that works best for us all together."

We groan simultaneously. Only Rachael would be excited to study and learn. Rayne voices our collective opinions. "Great, back in school again. You know we are on summer break, right? We aren't supposed to have to study again for a couple of months."

We laugh but the adults don't see the humor. Landon's mom, Lydia, crosses her arms over her chest and raises an eyebrow. "Would you rather wait until you are attacked and then try to figure out a way to work together?"

CHAPTER 16

After hours of practicing, we are no closer to being able to work together than when we started. Landon, Penelope, Chase and I have no problem working together. Rayne and Ethan have no problem working together. Whenever we try to mix the two, it explodes in our faces. Literally. The adults are having a good time watching from the deck. They think it is pretty funny each time we are thrown back and end up on our butts. We are frustrated.

At least after the first time were been smart enough to move away from the pool so none of us land in it. Although, I did get a good laugh when Rayne emerged spitting and sputtering, after she and Ethan were thrown in. I stopped laughing quickly when I was soaked too as a wave came up out of the pool and landed on my head. Then it was Rayne who was laughing. After a small water fight, try again to force our magick to work together. The harder we try the harder it resists. The adults don't understand this.

Landon's dad, Derek, tries to help. "Magick is not a

separate entity, it's a part of you. It's an extension of you. It can't resist working with the magick from someone else. You control it, not the other way around."

Rayne mutters, "Well, our magick didn't get that memo." We stifle our laughs as the adults are getting pretty frustrated with us.

Chase and Penelope's dad, Henry, gets up and walks over, "I have an idea. We are assuming your magick works the way that ours does. We have not been taking into account the ancient magick that has bonded with yours. It bonded with you four, and then later with Rayne and Ethan. You six have not bonded as a team to combine your magick. Therefore, every time you try to work together, your magick sees the other magick as a threat."

Lydia jumps up from her seat and walks over. We watch her cautiously. It is completely out of character for her to get this excited. "Landon and Penelope had to combine their magick, and so did Chase and Annisa before they could combine the magick of all four of them. Have you and Ethan combined your magick yet Rayne?" She asks directly.

We look over and are surprised by the sheepish expression on her face. Before she can respond, Renae interjects "Rayne has a few issues when it comes to this kind of thing. She has a hard time trusting her own instincts about her feelings. She is afraid someone else is making her feel what she is experiencing."

Rayne refuses to look directly at Ethan. He is visibly mad. She glares at us. "It's not my fault they manipulated me and my dad. I can't change the fact that the Council buried their thoughts in my head. And, I can't forget it. It cost my dad his sanity and eventually his life. How am I supposed to know if I am really feeling the emotions, or if it is a thought they planted? How do I know that this time is different?"

I can tell this is going to escalate to a fight if someone doesn't step in soon. Rayne is reacting like she is being ganged up on, and her reflex action to that type of situation is anger and lashing out. I look around at the others and make a quick decision. "I have an idea. The adults are going to have to stay here and trust us away from the house, though."

As I look at the adults, none of them seem concerned. I am a little confused because they have been trying to keep us here at the house since we moved in. My dad chuckles. "We trust you. Until we started to show the truth about you, it was simply not safe for you to leave the protection of the house. We wanted to make sure there wasn't going o be an angry mob coming to look for you. We know if the Advisors come after you now while you are out, you can take care of yourself."

Once again the parents point out a scenario that we hadn't considered. It makes sense, so I decide to let the matter drop. I turn to Rayne and Ethan, "You are just going to have to trust me on this. I think I know how to fix this."

Ethan nods his head. He has no problem with this. Rayne, however, studies me for a few minutes before she replies. "You better not be trying to get me to do some archaic ritual where we dance around in the woods naked, rubbing animal blood on ourselves."

"Do those actually exist?"

She groans and gestures for me to lead the way. Since my car has the third row seats, we pile in, and I pull out of the driveway. Chase looks over, "Where are we going."

"You'll see."

As we get close to the parking lot, everyone except Ethan has figured out where we are going. Rayne says from the back of the car with nervousness in her voice, "I'm not sure this is such a good idea. I don't have very many good memories from here. Actually, every memory from here has pretty much changed my whole life."

I don't say anything until I pull in the parking lot and turn the car off. I turn around in my seat so I can look Rayne in the eye as I tell her my plan, "I know this place is not somewhere you have ever felt safe. The problem is, when you were here before, you were not the same person that you are now. The last time you were here, you came to relive what had happened with your dad and you were by yourself. That is when the ancient magick read your soul, and deemed you good and trusted you with the most important job in our world, to protect the Origin.

You have doubted yourself ever since you realized you had been manipulated your entire existence. Believe me, I understand that doubt, and how violated you felt because we have gone through the same thing. The magick here is pure. It has not been contaminated by the will of others. All I am asking is that you walk out to the beach with Ethan, and listen to it."

She has tears in her eyes, but refuses to let them fall down her face. She nods her head and turns to Ethan. He smiles at her before clasping her hand and they get out of the car. Rayne looks over her shoulder at us, "Aren't you guys coming?"

We shake our heads. "This part is private and only meant for the two of you. Yes, we are a group and we will be bonded, but the strongest bond is between you and your soul mate. You are a separate entity from the group."

She nods her head in understanding. With one final look of hope, she turns, and walks down the trail holding hands with Ethan.

When they are out of site Penelope asks, "How long do we give them?"

I smile, "We'll know when to go to them."

The others give me a look of confusion. I don't know how I know. I just know this is what needs to be done.

After about a half hour we feel their magick combine. Landon starts to open his door and Penelope puts her hand on his arm to stop him. He looks back at her with confusion as Chase looks at her from his seat just as confused.

She just smiles, "Give them some time to enjoy it. Remember how it felt when we combined our magick as a couple?"

Understanding dawns in both their eyes and they settle back into their seats to wait a little longer. After another half hour we can feel that it is time to go. Without saying a word, we get out of the car and start walking down the trail that will lead us to the beach. When we reach them, Rayne and Ethan are both smiling. Rayne looks at me with astonishment. "Thank you! I can never repay you for what you did for us."

"All you have to do is be happy. Oh, and go back to being yourself, you being nice is really freaking me out."

Everybody laughs. I turn and start walking to the woods. I know everyone else will follow. When I reach the clearing where our final battle with Peter had taken place, I stop on the edge of the clearing and let the memories take over.

With tears flowing, I look at Rayne. "He was himself in the end. When I drained the magick out of him, the spells were broken. He thanked us for releasing him and warned us to be careful who we trusted. He said he was just the beginning, and the Council had back up plans. I want you to know he remembered who he was and he tried to help as much as he could. He also asked me to tell you how much he loved you. His final thoughts were of you."

She has tears streaming down her face as Ethan pulls her into his chest. As hard as it is to tell her about her father's final moments, she needs to know that he was himself at the end and that he loved her. We move to the center of the clearing while Ethan whispers comforting words to Rayne, who mourns the loss of her father. After a few minutes they join us. Her eyes are red and puffy from crying, but she doesn't say anything. After we stand there for a few minutes staring at each other Rayne can't suppress her smart-ass comments any longer. "So, what now, Oh, Great Wise One?"

It is nice for her to be acting more like herself, even as I was enjoying the break from her snarky comments. "I don't know. I know we need to bond and find a way to combine our magick, but I don't know the best way to go about doing it."

"So, you drag us out here in the middle of nowhere, make us take a hike through the woods without telling us beforehand, forcing me to ruin my shoes and then say, 'I don't know'?" she decries.

Before I can say anything, Chase defends me. "I don't remember you coming up with any bright ideas."

Just as Ethan is getting ready to say something to defend Rayne, we feel it. The ancient magick comes up from the ground begins filling each of us. As it makes its way through our bodies, it mixes with our own magick. While we stand in fascination, we watch as the magick pours out of each of us and starts swirling in the center of the circle we have formed without realizing it. It is a cyclone, gaining more and more power. Hovering above our heads.

It suddenly shoots back out to each of us. We are once again thrown back, landing on our butts. When we stand up, we can feel the magick and how it has changed. We can now feel the emotions of everyone there. The four of us jump when we hear Rayne's voice in our heads say, *"What the hell?"*

She looks at us in confusion not knowing why we jumped. I groan, and Penelope laughs. Chase looks between Rayne and me. "This won't end well."

Rayne is still completely confused, so I can't help myself. I speak directly into her mind. *"Not so funny when we know more than you is it?"*

She narrows her eyes at me. We hadn't told anyone about being able to do this so Rayne and Ethan were completely unprepared. Since she doesn't know how to control it yet, we hear the whole string of cuss words that run through her head. I laugh. "Impressive. I think I may have learned a few new words from that." I look at the others, waiting for them to agree with me.

Rayne figures out that we know what is going on, "Ok, what the hell happened? Did you do some weird spell to make it to where you are in my head or something? I will find a way to stop this." She says out loud.

Ethan turns her so she is looking at him, "I can hear every thought going through your head. I also heard when Annisa asked you if it was still funny. I don't think it would have worked like that."

She can see that he is right, but she isn't ready to let me off the hook yet. "So, what did you do then?"

Chase sighs. "She didn't do anything. When we combined our magick, it linked our minds too. We have been able to communicate like this for quite a while now. It is how we were able to coordinate and contain your temper tantrum at the football game last year. We can teach you how to only send the thoughts you want to send. You can also control who the thoughts go to, either the group as a whole, or only one or two. Frankly, I want to teach you both how to do that as quickly as possible, because if I have to keep listening to how sexy Ethan thinks you are when you are angry, I might throw up."

Ethan's face turns a bright red. Rayne looks over at him with a smirk as the rest of us laugh. We have been trying to ignore Ethan's thoughts. We know he can't control it, and probably doesn't realize that we can hear it. Once Ethan and Rayne fathom how hard it is to gain control, it takes their minds off of each other, and we are no longer trying to ignore the thoughts of what they want to do to each other. It makes the process more tolerable for us. Since each of us controls this aspect of our magick differently, it takes them a while to figure out what works best for them.

After a few hours of working on it, they are better able to control what thoughts they send out and who they send them to. We do manage to convince them that when practicing, it is better to use thoughts that don't have to do with sex since they keep sending to everyone. When we see Ethan blush for no apparent reason we know that they have figured out how to send thoughts to only where they want them to go.

Ethan looks back at us embarrassed as he notices us watching him. "Please tell me you guys did not see the picture she just sent to me."

Chase can't help his curiosity, and I groan when he asks, "No. Why, what was it?"

Ethan turns red again, but it is Rayne who answers with a grin. "It was a picture of me, and what I plan on doing to him later."

Chase is sorry that he asked, "Ok, I'm glad I didn't have to see that."

CHAPTER 17

Working on finding the best way to work together as a group goes a lot smoother after we return. Their way of doing things is completely different than ours. It takes us some time to figure out how to combine the two ways and find middle ground, but at least we aren't alone in this. The adults started working with us as soon as they deemed it was safe, and we weren't going to be thrown to the ground repeatedly. It is comforting to see they are struggling just as much as we are with trying to learn a new way to do things.

Once we figured out how to work as a team, and Rayne and Ethan stopped letting the occasional thought go out to the group, we need to start paying attention to the feelings. All of our emotions have been running high as we got frustrated and discouraged. It makes it worse that when we feel the frustrations of the other ones, increasing our own. We have to find a way to deal with sensing six people all the time.

We take a break from training and are floating in the pool soaking up the sun. We are obtaining some impressive tans from spending time outside practicing. Also, fewer things are broken if we are outside.

I can feel that everyone is relaxed so I think this will be the best time to bring it up. "We really need to talk about feeling each other's emotions."

I look over at Rayne and wait for her snarky comment. She doesn't disappoint. "Oh, please Wise One, enlighten us on how to keep this from happening."

"There is no way to keep it from happening. When it first happened with us, we had to learn to push the emotions of the others to the back of our mind. That way the only way they even registered was if they were feeling something strongly. Then we had to find a way to shove even the strong ones back, because that got awkward really fast."

Rayne starts laughing seeming to understand what I am saying but not saying, "Wait, are you telling me you could feel when the others were getting it on by their emotions?"

Landon replies flatly. "Yes, just like now we know that you and Ethan get it on every freaking night before you go to bed."

Ethan's face turns bright red and Rayne continues to laugh. "I bet that's been helping your sex lives. Wait, since I haven't gotten that vibe from any of you that must mean that you don't have sex lives."

The smirk leaves her face when I don't even raise my head from my float. "No, unlike you, we have learned not to broadcast to everyone."

"You can control the emotions that are sent out to the group?"

"No, but you can control how strongly they are going out. It became clear that it was necessary when the awkward moments the next morning became too uncomfortable."

Penelope tries to help. "Like right now, you are broadcasting your annoyance so strongly that it has made us annoyed. None of us are actually annoyed. We know you are not doing it on purpose, but your emotions are so strong that it drowns our emotions out and the only thing we can feel is your annoyance."

She actually sounds apologetic. "Ok, so how do I control how strongly they are broadcast?"

"That is hard to explain."

We take a few minutes to figure out how to say it to where they will both understand. Finally, Chase thinks he has an idea. "Ethan, it will be easier for you because your personality is laid back. You aren't aggressive nor trying to dominate."

Rayne opens her mouth to start yelling at Chase. Based on her emotions, she is really pissed. Chase holds his hand up. "Hold on Rayne. I'm not saying any of this to be mean or try to slam you. You have a talent for placing thoughts into a person's head. That is how the Council used you. It is second nature to you to be able to do this. While your power for that is something you have to consciously do, it is that very power that is trying to force your emotions on us. Put that together with your strong personality and it makes this a lot harder for you."

As Chase explains his theory we feel her calm down. She realizes he is right. "Ok, since I know how to control whether or not I place a thought, can I use those same techniques to soften my emotions so they're not screaming in your heads?"

We nod. It is the best we can explain what she needs to do. She thinks about it for a few minutes. We can feel when she tries to soften her emotions. It only takes her a couple of tries to figure out how to accomplish what she wants. We let out a collective sigh of relief as her emotions fade into the back of our minds.

She is annoyed by our obvious relief, but thankfully that annoyance is only a glimmer in the back of our minds. "It couldn't have been that bad to have my feelings in your head."

I raise an eyebrow. "Would you like it if you could feel one of our emotions all the time and not be able to enjoy a nice gesture your fiancé did for you, because someone else was irritated with her boyfriend and that was the only thing that you could feel?"

Her confidence astounds me sometimes. "That would never happen to me. I would never allow your emotions to overshadow mine."

I snort. I push a strong urge to smack her into her head and she smacks herself. "You were saying?"

Everyone laughs except Rayne, who is extremely annoyed with me. At least I can feel her annoyance only slightly. My float suddenly flips over, and I am plunged into the water. I come up sputtering. "It was totally worth it!" Now even Rayne is laughing.

We look up as the door to the house opens. We stop what we are doing and watch as Brian makes his way down to us looking miserable and lost. None of us know what to do, but suddenly the link is open between us. Surprisingly, it is Penelope that talks. *"We can't trust him. I know what it looked like, but I have a weird feeling when it comes to him. I don't think he would have done that just for show, but something isn't right."* We agree and wait to see what he wants.

He sits in one of the chairs beside the pool. "Hey, guys. Sorry to just barge in, but I really don't know what to do anymore. I have always had Amy and our parents, so I'm a little lost now. I didn't come here to talk about any of the stuff going on. I just wanted some friends to hang out with for a little bit."

I feel sorry for him. "There are some extra swim trunks in the pool house. Change into a pair and join us."

As soon as he is in the pool house Rayne lets me know how upset she is with me. "What part of don't trust him don't you understand?" She asks quietly.

I huff out a frustrated breath. "I'm not planning on giving him our deepest darkest secrets. As long as he sticks with not talking about anything that is going on and just hanging out, I don't see the harm in him spending an afternoon with people he had come to consider friends rather than wandering around lost."

"Not everybody is a project that you have to fix. Sometimes they are just playing you to get what they want.

Did you ever consider that this whole thing has been part of their plan?"

I am having a hard time figuring out how it would benefit them, but since my mind doesn't work like that, I can't expect to figure out a plan to hurt others. Brian comes back out of the pool house and grabs one of the extra floats sitting at the edge joining us in the cool water. "Wow, this feels great. I would love to have a nice cool pool to jump into on these hot days."

I smiled at him. "Yeah, it really is nice." I get the feeling that he is expecting a different reaction to that comment.

He looks a little disappointed, but I can't figure out why until Rayne explains it to me in my head. *"He was trying to get you to extend an open invitation. He wanted you to say something like, 'Feel free to come over anytime', so he would have an excuse to keep coming back. I am actually a little impressed you were able to resist your saintly urges and not say that. Oh, and just to be clear: Do. Not. Say. That."*

I send her a mental picture of me flipping her off. She laughs and Brian's head snaps up to look at her like she is crazy while everyone else suddenly looks nervous. She covers well. "Brian, you just missed Annisa being dumped off of her float into the water. It was great. You should have seen the look on her face."

I am able to give her the scowl I wanted to when she started laughing and not look suspicious. I firmly close the link in our heads so she would hear it slam down. She looks at me sideways through her sunglasses, but doesn't say anything or try to open it back up.

We lay on our floats and soak up some sun for a while, then Brian asks a question that has us very suspicious. "I thought with you guys having been here for so many lifetimes, there would be a place of power. I haven't been able to find one. Is there one here that I just haven't found yet?"

Chase doesn't even twitch. "Not that we've found. Why, are you looking for one? My parents mght be able to tell you where the closest one is since they have traveled so much."

"I just like the peace that I feel when I am in one. Right now, I could really use that connection. No big deal I was just wondering. So, what have you been doing so far over summer break?"

"You're looking at it. As you can tell from our awesome tans, we have been hanging out by the pool. Annisa and I are enjoying the calm before the storm that will start when we get into the full swing of wedding planning."

"I always thought the planning was left to the girls."

With that, the three girls dump water on him from the pool. A pretty massive water fight starts from there. It is impressive that none of us has to actually move to pelt anyone with water. I love this part of being a witch. When it calms down, Landon frowns at Brian. "You never say something like that when you have three girls who wield magick right here."

Brian laughs. "Yeah, I didn't think about that before I said it."

"We are so close that it will probably be the group of us planning this wedding. Chase and Annisa will want our thoughts on it too. For us, a wedding is a family affair."

Brian is thoughtful for a minute. "It sounds like you are going to be pretty busy for the next year focusing on the wedding. Hopefully, it won't distract you too much to be able to keep up at school."

None of us respond. I suddenly understand why he is here. He may have told Amy he was walking away, but now he has realized how hard it is to go on without your soul mate. He is here fishing for information he can use to get back in with the others. After about an hour, he gives up. "I should be going. Thanks for letting me hang out for a while. It was nice not to sit at home alone again all day."

Rayne glares at me. She knows it is killing me to not invite him to come over anytime. I manage to suppress it. "You're welcome. We'll see you later."

She raises her eyebrows, seemingly impressed that I am able to stifle my urges.

CHAPTER 18

That night, we tell the adults about Brian's visit. They agree with my assessment on why he was here. My mom gives me a sympathetic look. "Honey, I know it was really hard for you to not try and help him. I am very proud of you for being able to see what he was trying to do and not fall into the trap that he had laid. He has spent enough time around you, he knew that you would want to try to help him."

Rayne throws her hands in the air frustrated. "If she would just learn that not everybody needs her help, it would make things easier."

Renae turns to her daughter with an expression of annoyance. "And if you would learn that sometimes it is better to help someone, rather than watch them struggle needlessly, it would be nice."

Rayne lowers her eyes in shame. "I help when I think they deserve it. I helped these guys last year when I realized they were being manipulated. You're right that I didn't used to, but I have gotten better about it. I just don't jump to help everyone that crosses my path."

Renae has a sad look in her eyes. "I'm sorry. Sweetheart I didn't mean that the way it sounded. You're right. You have been helping people since you realized what was really going on. I just meant that you shouldn't immediately dismiss Annisa's urge to help someone. You need to look at the whole situation."

"I know. I get it mom. I'm working on it. I spent so many lifetimes thinking I was always the one that got screwed, and in a way, I was. I was never free to find Ethan, and I spent all that time creating problems that didn't need to be there. It's only been a couple of months. I am doing my best. It's hard to change your perspective."

Landon's dad attempts to make her feel better. "None of us have thought about it like that. You have gone through just as much as the rest of them. It is amazing you are doing as well as you are after your whole existence has been turned inside out."

Rayne is obviously starting to get uncomfortable with being the topic of conversation. "So Annisa, who is going to be your maid of honor?"

I gladly help her obvious change of topic. "I thought Penelope would be my maid of honor, and you would be my bridesmaid. I want a small wedding party and I thought that would be perfect."

Chase takes my hand in his. "That works for Landon to be my best man and Ethan to be my groomsman too."

Penelope and Rayne both stare with tears in their eyes. They speak at the same time. Penelope asks, "You want me to be your maid of honor?

Rayne whispers, "You want me to be in your wedding?"

I laugh. "Of course I do. Penelope, I couldn't think of a better maid of honor. You have been with me through all of this, you let me come to my own conclusions, and have never held it against me that this kept you from being with Landon. Rayne, you are a part of our family now. It wouldn't be right if you weren't up there with us too."

They both get up and come over to give me hugs, the tears now streaming down their faces. The guys watch us as if we have gone insane. Landon turns to Chase. "Dude, I'm not going to cry, but I would be honored to be your best man."

Ethan chuckles. "I'm not going to cry either, but I am also honored to stand up with you."

We narrow our eyes at them, but it is Rayne that tells them what we are all thinking. "Leave it to the guys not to know this is an emotional decision and must be treated as such."

Without missing a beat Ethan counters. "Leave it to the girls to blow it way out of proportion and get all weepy about it."

I smirk at Rayne. "Looks like you might have met your match."

Everyone laughs at her stunned expression. Directing her narrowed her eyes at him, she decides to let it go when he just grins at her. I can tell it is going to get interesting around them. Penelope moves on. "Now that we know what Brian is up to, what do we do? He didn't really get any information out of us, so he won't have anything to take to them to get back in, but I don't think he really needs it. I think he is able to walk back to them and pick right up where he left off. The question is, will he?"

I only think about it for a second. "He definitely will. I wouldn't be able to walk away from Chase and stay away."

Rayne asks her mom, "What do you think?"

Renae had walked away from her soul mate, and their daughter, when the Council had messed with their heads so much that they were not the same people anymore. We can tell she is heartbroken remembering. "He will go back to her. I would have gone back to Peter if he hadn't been driven insane. Even with how much he and Rayne had both changed, I almost went back many times. The only thing that kept me away was knowing I might have to stop them myself if it came down to it. I couldn't watch as they were turned into murderers. I couldn't stand by and let them hurt innocent people, but I didn't have the strength to do what needed to be done. I left so I wouldn't have to make that choice.

It wasn't until Rayne found me that I realized I had decided. I chose to turn my back, which was the same thing as standing there watching them hurt people. I was allowing it to happen by not doing anything. I was so ashamed. It is why I didn't immediately have Rayne come live with me. I couldn't face her. How could I have walked out on her, and let them keep doing this to her? I was supposed to protect her. Walking away was not just the hardest thing I have ever done, it was also the most cowardly and selfish.

Brian isn't like me though, he wants to make things right. He also doesn't know yet who he is without her. He is so young. This is not a decision he can make and stick to. It really isn't a question of 'if' he will go back, but 'when'. That is why the Advisors left him here in the first place. They knew he would be back. As long as Amy didn't go with him, they wouldn't be able to keep him away."

We sit in stunned silence and let her words sink in. None of us had been expecting her to be so candid about her experience. It is at that moment that I realize we truly are a family. This is how it feels to be in a family, we trust each other so much that we can tell each other these things about ourselves and know that they will still love us after they know.

I study the others and see the same realization dawning in their eyes. I happen to be looking at Rayne when I see the exact moment she accepts that she is part of a real family. She has never had that before. It is the first time in her existence that she knows where she actually belongs. She notices me watching her, nods her head showing that she accepts this, but refuses to give it anymore acknowledgment than that.

I understand this is hard for her. She is finally part of a family but her dad is not in it. I watch my dad and know that

I would have been devastated if he had been in Peter's position. I have a new respect for Rayne. What she did to help us against her father is something that not many people would be able to do. I don't want to make things more uncomfortable for Rayne or Renae. They have experienced their share of awkward conversations for the night.

"We need to figure out what our next move is. We have exposed the Advisors, but I have a feeling that what happened was part of their plan. I think they wanted to look like the bad guys so they could prepare without the others constantly looking to them for guidance. It will also make them look like the heroes when the Council has been destroyed, and they accept the position even though everyone doubted them."

Chase stares at me in shock. "I can't believe that just came out of your mouth. Are you feeling alright? You never even think of the bad in people. For you to say that is just not right."

I let out an exasperated sigh. "Just because I always try to find the good in people doesn't mean that I can't see the bad. I usually just choose not to dwell on the bad. Unfortunately, this time I don't have a choice."

Chase and Landon both laugh at the pained expression on my face as I say this. "Just because I don't have a choice doesn't mean I have to like it."

Penelope takes the focus off of me and my uncharacteristic description of our situation. "Annisa's right, I felt like something was off with Brian when he got here earlier. As soon as I saw him, I knew we couldn't trust him. Something is not right with the way that he walked away from Amy. The whole scene at the engagement party felt off to me."

We give her a weird look. "What didn't you feel it too?"

We shake our heads. None of us had gotten that feeling.

Henry smiles. "Penelope it looks like we just discovered your talent, and it is going to come in very handy."

We look at him like he has lost his mind.

"You sense deception. All witches can sense if they are being lied to. The problem is, as long as the person is telling some version of the truth, or the truth as they see it, you won't feel the lie. It also only works if it is a conversation between small groups. It doesn't work in a public setting. The others were not able to hear the lie Danny was telling because he was making it as a public announcement and not telling just a few people. You Penelope, are able to sense deception no matter the setting. The person doesn't have to be talking directly to you or a group that you are in.

All you have to do is hear what they are saying, and you will know if there is deception in their intent. The twist is, even if the person that is doing the deceiving doesn't realize that is what he is doing, you will still sense it. I have a feeling that poor Brian had a spell on him that caused him to react the way he did at the engagement party. He didn't realize he was deceiving anyone, but there was still a deception there, so you were able to sense it.

When the spell wore off the next day he realized he never really wanted to do it in the first place. The reason you felt like you couldn't trust him when he walked up today was because he came here with the intent of getting information he could take back to the Advisors. My guess is, as soon as he left here, he went back to them and told them how distracted you were going to be planning the wedding. It was smart to plant that seed. They will think they have the perfect opportunity while you are busy planning the wedding."

I interrupt him at this point. "I really don't want to use our wedding as a ploy to trick someone, I would rather our wedding not be associated with this in any way."

My mom is the first one to reassure me. "Honey, we aren't going to use the wedding or the planning of the wedding for this. A wedding is a sacred and very special occasion. We would never even think about tarnishing that. What he is saying, is they will think you are distracted by the wedding when in truth you won't be. Yes there is a lot to plan, but we have a whole year. We will be able to space out what needs to be done so that it isn't piled on you all at once. You will have plenty of time for each decision and the stress will be minimized."

Chase takes my hand. "Baby, I promise you that you will have the wedding of your dreams." He looks at my mom. "We were not joking when we said that the wedding is a family affair. We all will be involved in planning the wedding. You will not be doing it on your own."

My mom grins. "I'm very glad to hear that."

CHAPTER 19

We decide that as the Advisors are preparing, so should we. We meet up with all the adults, and surprise them with the questions that we have. Even though Penelope has her memories, there is still some information, none of us know.

"We have made a good start toward redeeming ourselves, but to continue on that path there is some important information we need. Specifically how we came to be, and how everyone came to see us the way that they do. I know they had plenty of reasons to resent us for the way we were acting, but it feels like there is more to it."

The adults share a look that confirms I am right. They haven't been telling us something. I can also tell from the look, that it is time for us to know. I sense there is a mutual diversion from them though that they don't want to be the one to tell us.

My dad sighs and starts. I soon realize that even though I had asked, I really didn't want to know. "You know everything we do is a give and take. We take the power from the land for our magick and use the energy around us to fuel that magick. For everything that we take, we must give an offering back. For example, when we use the energy of the plants around us, we then water and trim those same plants, and take care of them in the ways that they can't care for themselves. When you use Magick from the Origin, it takes a bigger payment. You share your magick with the Origin, so not only is the Origin boosting your power, but you are boosting its power as well. The reason the six of you have been claimed as Guardians of the Origin is because you have been, and are continuing to use the power. That is your payment and for the use of the power. You can use what you need, but in return you have to protect the Origin and keep it safe."

I glance at Chase and see he feels the same way that I do. "I think we can agree that is not too high of a price. I have no problem with that payment."

The others nod their heads in agreement.

Penelope is the one to speak for all of us. "It feels like that is not enough of a payment, there should be more. I understand protecting the Origin is important, but we are not alone in that. The Origin has its own protection spells. Actually, It does most of the work."

My mom sighs. "We were hoping to wait a few years before getting into this, but you are more perceptive than we thought. In order to understand this, we need to explain more about how we came to be. We told you the Origin created the Council, and they created the rest of us, but we didn't get into detail about how that was done. You remember I told you about how normal people that have discovered the magick around them can use it, right?" She leans forward looking at each of us. "Well, at one point, all of us were like that too. The Origin chose three people that were strong in their belief, and very skilled with using the magick, and that is who they initially instilled the power in. That is how the Council was created.

The Council then searched the world for people who

were worthy of being instilled with this power. They would bring those people into the Origin, and if the Origin agreed they were worthy, they would be instilled with the power. No new soul has ever been created. You four were very strong and the Advisors saw the opportunity to use you to get what they wanted. They talked the Council into bringing you to the Origin, but they didn't realize that the Origin could feel their intent. That is why you were allowed to be given so much power. The Origin has the ability to read a person, not just their magick. It can determine the intent in which you will use the power given to you.

Not everyone the Council brought to the Origin was given the gift. Some were turned away and their memories altered to not remember the experience. The Origin can also hide memories so far in your mind that you will never find them. When the Origin gave you four power, it was not so you could protect the Council like they believed. It was so you could protect the Origin itself. It could tell what the Advisors were planning and it wanted to protect those it had created.

Once our souls are instilled with power, it creates a new being. Our personalities are still the same, but our makeup is altered. That is why we don't go through the same mortal cycle that normal people do. They live a life and go to heaven. They create new souls when they get pregnant, where we have to be implanted with the soul of one of our own. We can't make a new soul by having a baby.

There is only one exception to that rule, the six of you. You original four have always had the ability to create new souls. When the Origin gave the power to Rayne and Ethan to make them guardians as well, it changed their makeup enough to give them this ability as well. You have to be vigilant in using birth control, because you can get pregnant just as normal people do, and you don't have to wait for the Council to approve you having a baby and instilling a soul within you. Your children's Soul Mates will be a complicated issue and something we discuss later."

I can't help but interrupt her. There is something about this that I don't understand. "As interesting as this is, I don't understand how this has anything to do with the payment we will have to give. I understand how important the information is, but I don't get how it ties in to what we are talking about."

My mom waits to make sure that was all I am going to ask before she continues. "I was getting to that. The payment you have to give is your children."

We jump up and Penelope is the first one to get out what we are thinking, each of us prepared to throw a fit. "We didn't agree to that. That is a price that we will not pay. We will find another way and not use the Origin or its power."

My mom stands up and grabs my arms. She forces me to look at her as she continues. "You are misunderstanding what I mean. You don't have to give up your children, and nobody is going to take them. You have to train them to be Guardians. You get to raise them in the way that you see fit, nobody will interfere with you being the parents. The payment is that your children will be Guardians after you no longer can. Your bloodlines are now the Guardian Bloodlines. Magick may be in the soul and not the bloodline, but the Guardians will be from bloodlines."

I am still in shock. I turn to Landon. "Do you understand what this means? Only our families will be the ones with the honor of guarding the Origin."

He frowns. "I don't like the idea of having to tell them they can't do anything else, or they are stuck because we promised it for them."

Rayne smirks. "Good luck telling that to any of my kids."

I groan. "Can't we have one conversation without your smart-ass comments? I get it you don't like it."

Penelope interrupts before the bickering escalates. "It is pointless to argue about it now. The deal has already been made. We can't back out of it now."

Mom jumps back in the conversation. "It is the price that is due, but it is not a burden, it is an honor. Your children and their children after them will be in the honorable bloodline of the Guardians. They will not be hurt and you will still be the parents."

I reply. "Ok, I can live with that. I think that is fair. It is not something that will hurt our kids, but will actually help them. We can teach them the responsibility from a young age so we don't overwhelm them. The hard part will be trying to teach them without telling them about the magick until they are 16."

My dad interrupts this time. "Um, that won't be necessary. Your kids will be new souls. They will not be bound by the same rules the rest of us are. They will have their powers at birth. You will be able to begin to teach them about the use of magick and their responsibility to the Origin as soon as they are old enough to understand. Just remember, they will have the power of the Origin from birth as well. It will not be as powerful as what you have, the Origin will limit what they can do until they are old enough to understand what that power means, and what it can do. The hardest part will be trying to teach them to control it, and keep them from showing others what they can do. Kids naturally want to show off and show others. what they can do."

It really is a give and take. We get to have children and they will be ours, not a soul instilled within us, but we have to train them, and they must become Guardians. We also have to basically hide our children until they are old enough to understand that they can't let anyone know what they can do. It is a lot to take in.

Chase can see I am struggling with this new information. He tries to comfort me. "Baby, it's not as hard as you think. Penelope had her magick from birth, and I grew up with her being able to do all this stuff. As long as we are open with them and teach them, it will be fine. We have to explain it to them in a way that they understand. You will not be as isolated as you think. Penelope and Rayne will be mothers dealing with the same thing as you. We are in this together."

I look over at Rayne and Penelope and see a shared look

of relief. They had been feeling just as overwhelmed as I was. We feel a lot better about it when we realize that we will all be doing this together. Relief floods me. "The kids won't be isolated. They will have to know how to work together, so we will have to raise them together. Not only will their bond be strong to the Origin, but they will have a strong bond with each other. I think this might actually be a good thing. They will always have each other, so they will never feel like they are alone."

Rachel smiles at me, "I will be there too. Remember, I had to deal with the same thing with Penelope. I can give you tips on things that I did that worked."

I hadn't thought about it that way. I am feeling a lot better about the whole situation now.

Chase looks over at me. "As much as this is helpful information, we are not planning on having children for quite a few years yet, so how does this help us in our current situation?"

Henry laughs. "Nobody is saying that you have to have children right now, so you don't have to look so terrified. We are just letting you know that the Origin is helping you, and how the payment will work. We want you to understand what is at stake. You need to redeem yourselves to the other witches, but you have to be careful how you accomplish that. You can't reveal too much. You can't let them know that it is more than a place of power assisting you."

Landon has been quiet up until now, listening and taking everything in. "I think it's going to be harder than we think. We can't just barge in with power full force. We have gotten used to throwing our power out there to control the situation. We won't be able to do that against the Advisors without everyone knowing something is not right. They know we are powerful, and that we were created to be bodyguards for the Council, but if we show them the amount of power we have, it could have the opposite effect of what we want, showing them that we can take over if we want. It will make them fear us even more. We need to figure out a diplomatic way to do this."

I consider his words. "I see what you're saying, and I think you're right. I think it will be better to somehow strip them of their power over the Council and the other witches. We can't take their magick away, but we can take the power they think is the most important. If we can bring them down to the level of the rest of us, it will show that we don't want to just go in and do whatever is necessary to get what we want. It will show that we also take others into consideration."

Rayne is shaking her head at me. I am not surprised she disagrees with me. I am surprised by what she disagrees with. "I agree but knocking them down a few pegs won't work. They will just start scheming and manipulating, trying to work their way back up to that position of power. We will have to find some way to bring them down and discredit them, to the point where they can never return to their current positions."

We process what she said. Everyone is watching me to see how I will react. They know me well enough to know it is something I really don't want to do. My first instinct is to help people, not harm them. I can see that what Rayne is saying is the only way to proceed. I am resigned to our fate. "You're right Rayne. It is our only option."

Everyone stares at me with their jaws on the ground. "I can be reasonable! You don't have to look so shocked."

CHAPTER 20

The next day, we are trying to figure out what we are going to do when the doorbell rings. I am surprised to see Brian standing there. He smiles and asked if he can come in. Gesturing for him to follow me, I lead him into the living room where everyone else is gathered. As soon as I walk in, I glance over at Penelope. She shakes her head so slightly that if I were not watching for it, I would have missed it. He is here for reasons other than what he is about to tell us.

He smiles at everyone. "Hi, guys. Hope I'm not interrupting anything, but I thought I would stop by and give you some information. I thought I could be of some help if you want it."

Landon narrows his eyes but doesn't say anything. I can sense that the adults are outside the door, but we can't see them. They must have been on their way here when they heard Brian and decided to wait outside and see what he has to say.

Chase looks at him and I can see in his eyes that he doesn't trust Brian, but he doesn't let it show on his face or his voice, "What kind of information?"

If Brian knows that we don't trust him, he doesn't let it show. He sits down in a chair as I go back to the couch next to Chase. "I was thinking about it, and I think I can really help you. I can answer some of the questions I'm sure you have about the Advisors, and I can tell you how they work and give you an idea of what to expect."

Penelope again gives a very slight shake of her head. He is not telling us the whole truth. Landon has a strange expression on his face and it is making me wonder what he's thinking about. I will have to wait to ask though until we have dealt with Brian. Chase takes over as spokesperson for our group since each of us are so distracted. "Why would you suddenly want to help us? I can see that you are desperate to have someone to talk to since Amy is not here, but why would you help us instead of going back to her?"

My jaw drops and my eyebrows rise up. I can't figure out why he is pushing this. He has his mind tightly closed so I can't figure out what he is thinking, but I can feel that his emotions are steady. He is not doing this out of anger or frustration. The only thing I can think of is that he has a plan.

I am even more surprised when Brian responds. "I am going back to Amy. I talked to her yesterday. I am going back, but they asked me to come here and see what I could find out about what you know about them."

As soon as the words are out of his mouth, he stands up and looks around in a panic. He starts to stammer, but no actual words come out. He ultimately puts his hand over his mouth as he turns and walks out of the room. As soon as we hear the front door close, the adults come into the room looking very amused.

I look over at them and ask, "What just happened?"

Landon looks at me. "Don't you think we should tell them before they can answer that?"

I chew on my bottom lip with my brow furrowed. "They have been standing in the hall since Brian came in here. They heard everything. Didn't you feel them out there?"

Everyone shakes their heads at me. Landon doesn't notice. "I was too distracted by the fact that I knew there was a strategy to him being here. He came with a plan and didn't just stop by."

Derek finally takes pity on us. "I know what is going on. I figured you would exhibit the signs within a couple of days. Penelope found her talent for being able to sense deception. When that surfaced, it wasn't going to be long before the rest of you started showing signs of what your talent is.

Landon, you have a talent for being able to sense when someone has a plan. You are able to sense when someone has a strategy of his or her own.

Annisa, you have a talent for sensing other witches, and when a witch is near. You will be able to tell where they are and how many are there. I'm not sure how close they need to be for you to sense them, we will have to wait and see what your range is.

Chase, yours is the best and the worst talent. You have the talent to compel the truth. You don't even have to try. If you ask someone a direct question, they will answer with the truth before they realize they're speaking. That's why Brian answered your questions so truthfully, and then instantly left. As soon as he realized he was telling you the truth without meaning to, he left before he could reveal anymore."

We look at him in shock, until Rayne speaks, which leads to everyone directing shocked looks to her. "That must mean that my talent is being able to sense the intent of harm. As soon as he walked in the room, I could tell that he was here with the intention of harming us. I could also tell that he had no intention of harming us now, but in the future."

Derek smiles at her. "I wondered which one of you would have that talent. You see, there are specific talents that the Guardians will have. Which means Ethan has a talent for sensing bonds. When he is around two people, he will be able to sense how strong their bond is to each other. That will help when you start to deal with other witches. You will be able to tell if there is a possibility of splitting up a group and breaking it down until it is easier to work against, or if their bond is too strong for that."

I suddenly have a thought that I am surprised hasn't occurred to any of us before now. "How do you know all of this?"

My mom laughs. "I wondered how long it would take for one of you to ask that. Just as you know how to use your magick and what spell someone is using, we know what information you need. The Origin is able to give us the information that will be helpful for you when you as a question. It would have thrown off the balance for the Origin to give you this additional knowledge after it had given you so much power. It worked around that by giving us the information. We have the option of telling you, letting you figure it out for yourselves, or just keeping the information to ourselves. That keeps the balance in check."

"Ok, I get that, but how do we know if you are not telling us something? I don't like that you could have information that could help us, but have decided that it was something that you were not going to tell us." I frown as I think about how that could be bad for us in the future.

My mom smiles at me. "I understand what you are saying, but you are going to have to trust us. There is some information that we have kept from you because you were not ready to hear it, or we felt it was best for you to learn it on your own. We would never keep important information from you, no matter how hard it is for us to tell you, or for you to hear. We have already given you information we would rather not. We want to protect you and keep some of the bad away from you, but we realize that you have to deal with the bad before it becomes so big that you won't be able to do anything about it. Believe me, there is so much I would rather you not have to deal with, but because you don't have a choice but to deal with it, we are going to give you everything we can to help you through it."

I feel bad for doubting them. "I'm sorry, I didn't mean to sound like you were keeping stuff from us on purpose. It's just frustrating to know someone has more information about what we need to do."

Lydia joins the conversation. "We understand your frustration. We get frustrated with this too. There are times we want to tell you something, but we know it is better if you figure it out yourselves. Sometimes the steps it takes for you to discover the answers are the most important. The things that happen in the process, can be more important than the actual answer."

Rayne answers with her usual attitude. "So, basically, you know what we need to know, but you don't tell us for our own good. Why do I feel like I am two years old again?"

Renae laughs. "You always were impatient. At least you don't throw as many temper tantrums as you did at two."

Rayne narrows her eyes at her mother and we all laugh. Ethan steers the conversation back to where it needs to be. "So, if we are all finding our talents and how useful they can be, we need to start preparing for whatever it is the Advisors have planned. We may not agree with the Council and feel that they are corrupt, but we can't let the Advisors go through with their plan to overthrow them. We will have to protect them. We can deal with them and their agenda later, but the most dangerous threat right now is the Advisors."

We nod our heads in agreement. Chase then asks "Back to square one, how do we go about doing that?"

We spend the afternoon all giving and discarding different ideas. After hours of this, everyone is frustrated. Rayne's usual snarkiness surfaces. "So, we are the most powerful of our kind, and we have been given the job of protecting the Origin, and the other witches, and we can't figure out a way to put the power hungry Advisors in their place. This is going to be a disaster."

Chase groans in frustration. "It takes time to figure these things out sometimes. We can't just snap our fingers and have whatever we want."

While he says that, he snaps his fingers to prove a point, but the point is lost as a plate full of sandwiches appears. We stare at it with disbelief, but the adults burst into laughter.

Henry calms down enough to try to explain. "I guess you were hungry. Looks like you prepared enough for all of us. I am pretty hungry myself, so thanks."

We turn to him with brows raised and lips pressed together wondering if he has gone insane. Rachel takes pity on us and explains. "When your emotions are high, your magick will respond to that. Your magick could sense that you were frustrated and trying to figure out an answer, so when you thought about how easy it would be to just snap your fingers to get what you wanted, your magick tried to help and gave you something that you wanted. You have to remember how powerful you are. Your magick will do everything it can to help you. Each of you have to make sure that when you are frustrated, angry, or your emotions are high for any reason, that you pay attention to your magick to control it."

We decide that taking a break and eating is probably a good idea. Maybe after we have stepped back and gathered our thoughts in order, we will be able to come up with some new ideas instead of trying to make the old ones work somehow.

CHAPTER 21

The sun isn't over the horizon yet when I wake the next morning. It is starting to lighten up outside, but not enough to be a reason for me to rise. It takes me a minute to realize that I can sense a witch outside the house. Chase doesn't notice as I quietly slip out of bed. I make my way down to the main floor silently. I don't want to wake anybody else, and I don't want whoever is outside to figure out that I am up.

When I get to the bottom of the stairs, I close my eyes and concentrate to feel where the other witch is. It is the first time I am consciously using this ability and I'm not sure how to control it. I take a couple of deep breaths and focus on the new feeling. I locate the source in my core. I can feel my body tingling as I am urged to go to the back yard. I am surprised to feel that there is only one witch outside. I make my way through the house and out the back door.

I stay in the shadows, thankful that I had worn black shorts and a dark tank-top to bed. I don't stand out in the darkness, but blend in. I can see someone moving around out in the yard, but I am not close enough to be able to tell what they are doing. I want to get closer, but I also want to make sure that I have help if I need it. I stay on the porch, hidden in the shadows, and gently nudge Chase with my mind. After a minute I can feel his panic as he realizes I am not in bed and am trying to talk to him in his head.

He instantly starts firing questions at me. *"Where are you? Are you alright? What happened? Where do I need to come to find you?"*

I wait until he is done. He will not be able to hear me over his panic until he stops talking. *"Relax. I am just outside on the back porch. Don't make any noise, and don't turn on any lights. I woke up and sensed another witch outside the house. There is only one, but they are out in the yard doing something. I am going to try to get closer to see if I can figure out what they are doing. Be very quiet, wake the others, then wait in the kitchen. Remember, don't make any noises and don't turn on any lights. I won't be able to figure out what they are up to if they realize we are awake and run off."*

I feel the relief flood through him and I can tell he is doing as I asked. I focus again on the person who is currently looking at the ground in front of a little shed that holds the gardening tools. I stay in the shadows as much as possible as I make my way through the yard. Using bushes and trees to help hide me, I finally get close enough to see it is Amy. I still can't figure out what she is doing. Just as I move out from behind a tree to get a closer look, she turns to look at the house. I am not able to get back behind the tree before she sees me.

She wears a smirk on her face. "I didn't think you went anywhere alone. I am surprised you didn't wake everyone up in the house to come charging out here. You might be getting too cocky. Not everyone will just bow down to you and do what you want, I won't let that happen. I won't let you take over everything. You may want all the power, but we aren't going to sit back and let you destroy everything that we have worked for."

I cross my arms over my chest, purse my lips and raise my eyebrows. I don't want to let my anger keep me from figuring out what she is doing here. I narrow my eyes at her. "You have no idea what you are talking about. Have you ever thought maybe you are wrong about us? Have you noticed that not once have we tried to go after the Council? Or that we are just trying to live out our lives, and we have no intention of trying to take anything over?"

She sneers at me. "Yeah, like I'm going to believe that. You will say whatever you have to trying to convince us you are just trying to help. Then, when you have the support you want, you will make your move. I won't be fooled, I will stop you."

I realize that no matter what I say, I am not going to change her mind. Even after spending time with us, and seeing what kind of people we are, she is still solid in her belief that we are the bad guys. I decide to change tactics since this is not going to get us anywhere. "What are you doing out here? There has to be a reason you are sneaking around our yard before dawn. You obviously aren't here to attack since you are being careful not to wake any of us and are trying to make sure nobody saw you."

She smirks again. "Why would I tell you what I was doing? I'm not going to let you know what we know about your plan, or make things easier for you. You think I am just going to roll over and let you destroy my family and my whole way of life? You can't really be that stupid, can you?"

While she is talking I can feel the others quietly making their way through the yard toward us. I keep her focused on me so she won't notice them. When she has finished speaking, Rayne steps out of the shadows. "I'm pretty sure it's you who is the stupid one. You're the one that blindly believes what she is told without anything to back it up. Then, when you have some verification of the truth finds a way to twist it in your head so it's not real."

Amy snarls at her. "You have a lot of room to talk. You are a traitor. You are actually helping the people that killed your father for no reason. He was trying to protect us. They killed him, and you got all cozy with them. I don't know how you can live with yourself."

Ethan comes out of the shadows, angry about what Amy has said. He is not about to let Rayne take that kind of thing. She doesn't need his help though. Amy made a huge mistake. She has pissed Rayne off on a personal level. I almost feel sorry for Amy when I see the expression on Rayne's face. I can't hold on to that sympathy for more than a few seconds though. Amy brought it on herself.

Rayne speaks in a deceptively calm voice that does not match her emotions of pure rage. "*Your* family and *Their* schemes drove my father, who was a good man that just wanted to help keep the peace, insane. They manipulated him and messed with his mind so much that he became just a shell of himself, and a weapon. You, and everyone associated with that plan, is the traitor. You are more responsible for my father's death than anyone living in this house. Maybe we should help your father down the same path to become insane. Then you would know how it feels to just want him to stop suffering, want to do everything possible to bring the man that you love back again, but when you realize that he is so far gone that there is no way to save him or bring him back, I will give you the option of helping him by doing something you never thought you would be able to do, or sit back and watch him spiral deeper into insanity."

The more that Rayne talks, the more color that Amy's face loses. By the time Rayne has finished, there is no doubt in anyone's mind she has not made an empty threat. She would go through with what she is telling Amy if given the smallest opening and reason. The fact that she says this with a calm voice and conviction leaves Amy so shocked that she can't do anything but stare at Rayne for a minute.

Amy decides that she is going to try and play it off like she is not threatened. She holds her head high. "You can tell all the lies you want. I will not be fooled. You will not win. We will stop you." She turns and runs off.

We don't follow her. We need to figure out what was been doing here. Before we can even start to look, Rayne turns to me. "You need to learn how to be sneaky. If you hadn't let her see you, we could have figured out what she was up to."

I raise a brow. "You need to learn how to use that filter that keeps every thought that pops into your head from coming out of your mouth."

She pretends to think about that for a minute. "Nope, I don't have one of those."

I ignore the comment and move on. "We need to figure out what she was trying to do out here. What did you guys sense?"

Penelope speaks first. "I could sense the deception, but it wasn't in what she was saying. She truly believes everything that she said. Whatever it was she was doing, she was trying to keep us from figuring it out."

Landon is next. "There was a plan for her to be here. It was not an impulsive move. She definitely was here for a specific reason."

Rayne is thoughtful. "She definitely had the intent to harm us, but it was not tonight. I don't know what she was trying to accomplish, but she didn't intend for it to harm us now. Whatever it was, the harm comes later."

I look at Chase. "Too bad you didn't get a chance to ask her what she was up to before she ran off."

Ethan interrupts before Chase can answer. "I think we need to check around and see if we can find anything that might give us an answer to what she was doing. There was a reason she was here, and there was a reason she didn't want us to know that she was here."

I tell them what I had seen. Since she had been looking at the ground we decide that is the best place to start. When we get to the spot in front of the gardening shed where she had been standing something is not right. It doesn't look like the ground has been dug up, but something is not right with it. We try to figure out what is wrong.

After a minute, Rayne starts to laugh. We watch her with worried looks on our faces, starting to wonder if something is wrong with her. When she is finally able to get her laughter under control and sees the worried looks on our faces she decides to share what she thinks is so funny.

"I can't believe that none of us thought of this before, especially Ethan or I. The reason the ground doesn't look right, but doesn't look like it was dug up, is because she used magick to put something in it. It wouldn't be modern technology, the earth won't accept something like that without a sign. It has to be something that originally came from the earth so the earth will accept it back."

Ethan's eyes light up. He understands what Rayne is saying and he knows what it is. Before he explains to the rest of us, he concentrates on the area of grass that is not quite right. Then all of a sudden, a crystal comes up and rests on the grass. The grass under it now looks like it did before. You would not be able to tell that it had been tampered with.

I reach down to pick it up, but Ethan puts a hand on my arm to stop me. He makes eye contact with each of us to make sure he has all of our attention. "Do not touch these with your bare hands. This is tektite. It is a grounding stone. It naturally draws power into the earth. It is used to weaken or drain the power of another. It will work without us touching it if there are enough placed around us. If you touch it, it will instantly begin to draw your power from you.

We need to get some cloths to wrap them in. Then we need to spell a chest to contain their power, and we can take the chest and bury it somewhere. It is the only way to keep them from draining the power from others. It has to be placed with the intent of drawing the power for it to be at its most powerful. We will have to search the whole yard to find all of them. It won't be difficult now that we know what we are looking for. We can focus our magick in locating them."

She must have been out here for awhile, because there are a lot of them. It takes all of us working for a couple of hours to collect them all. After we have disposed of them, we sit down and explain to our parents what happened. They don't seem surprised. Rose gets up and walks out of the room. She comes back with a felt sack, sits back down, and starts pulling necklaces. They all have a beautiful stones with black and mahogany stripes and swirls. She gives one to each of us. The adults each have one also.

Seeing our confusion, she explains. "These necklaces are something that you need to wear all the time. We have been working on them for a while. We wanted to make sure we put enough energy and good intent in them to be powerful enough for all of us. The stone is mahogany obsidian. It will remove energy blockages including psychic cords that sap your inner strength, will offer protection from psychic attacks, and will strengthen your auras."

From the others faces, I know I am not the only one confused. "I thought obsidian blocked magickal abilities."

"What is a psychic cord?" Penelope asks at the same time.

The adults smile and Rose explains. "You can't believe everything that you read in books. There are a lot of misconceptions when it comes to crystals and stones. You have to know the properties and put good energy into them. Obsidian is a very quick acting protective stone. It acts as a shield against negativity, and absorbs negative energy from the environment."

Chase considers this. "That makes sense. Thank you. We will make sure that we always have them on."

Rose answers Penelope's question next. "Penelope, a psychic cord is a connection that is created when you interact with other people. Most of the time the cord is broken when the interaction is ended. However, If the other person feels they connected with you on a deeper level and feeds that connection then the cord becomes stronger and does not break. If you are not aware of the cord and do not take the appropriate action to consciously break the cord it can start to sap your energy."

I sigh. "There is so much we don't know that our enemies do. I always feel like we are trying to play catch up, and at a disadvantage."

My mom looks at me with sympathy. "I know it feels like that. But you have to remember, they will always underestimate you, which more than makes up for the lack of knowledge on your part. They may know more, but you have ability and skill they can not even imagine.

The rest of the day is a lesson on different crystals and stones, and what properties they hold. It is very interesting. I have a new respect for them and all that the earth has to offer to help us.

CHAPTER 22

We have to assume Amy knows we would find the tektite, and that they will know it is not working to drain our power. So, we have been on edge to see what they try next. We spend a lot of time going to nearby areas, trying to make peace with the other witches by helping where they need it. When we show up, they watch us with mistrust. After we have offered our services, helped them with their troubles, and asked for nothing in return, they are shocked. Some of them insist on us taking something in payment for helping, but we studiously refuse every time.

After a few trips, word gets out about what we have been doing. We are now getting letters and voicemails from people asking for our help, rather than threatening us. The more we are sought out, the better we feel about all of it. It looks like we are finally on the right path. We have a lot to atone for. We have behaved so poorly in every life and many innocent people were hurt. Even though our actions were not our fault, we feel responsible for the damage that was done. We may have been under a spell, but it doesn't change the fact that we did the magick that harmed.

During all of this, I can sense we are being followed. I assume it is Brian and Amy watching to see what we are up to, and how they can sabotage what we are accomplishing. They don't realize I know they are there. It works to our advantage. We help a group and after we leave, we circle back and fix whatever it is they are doing to sabotage our efforts.

At first the other witches are confused. They can't figure out why we would help and then it would fall apart, just before we would show back up to fix it again. It doesn't take them long to figure out that someone is coming behind us, trying to undo what we have done. Before long, there are extra people watching for the people responsible for the sabotage when we show up. Since the witches are being vigilant, Brian and Amy don't have a chance to act without being seen.

When I start to feel a larger group following us with more power, we know the Advisors have decided to do some of the work themselves. They don't expect what they find when they show up. We decide to hide in the forest around the property we just helped clean up after a flash flood destroyed the land. When the Advisors show up about an hour after we appeared to have left, they are surprised to find that they are not welcome.

They walk up to the door of the house, and it is opened before they have a chance to knock. They notice other witches come out from behind the barn where they had been working to build a new fence for the horses. The Advisors smile at the witches and as the land starts to fill with water again. They actually have a smug look on their faces. Danny steps forward as the leader speaks to the man who owns the property. "It looks like they only temporarily helped you. Of course, as soon as they are out of the area, all the water comes right back."

Danny is speechless as the man's wife glares at Claire. "If your wife would stop using her magick to bring the water back, it wouldn't be here."

Danny examines the faces around him, and sees the glares that he is getting from them. Claire instantly makes the water disappear again, obviously thinking it will help the situation instead of making it worse, which it does.

As soon as the water is gone, someone in the group that has been working on the fence voices his opinion. "Wow, those kids never said a word about being followed or someone sabotaging their work. They always just came back to check and make sure everything was alright, and would redo the work they had done in the first place. You just proved they are better people than you. While they never once said anything about you, or what you are doing, you came here and instantly tried to discredit them while doing something that is only meant to harm."

When Claire starts speaking, it is clear that Amy gets her personality from her mother. "You are going to believe the ones that have caused our problems have suddenly become trustworthy and helpful? Can't you see this is part of their plan? They are luring you in so that when they try to overturn the Council, you will go along, and actually help them."

To her surprise, the people around her start laughing. The four of them look around in confusion. When the group of witches realize that the Advisors have no clue what is happening, it makes them laugh harder. Finally, the witch who lives at that house is able to get his laughter under control. He addresses the four Advisors and voices what the Advisors never thought anyone would figure out.

"You have blamed four teenagers for trouble that you have created. This is not their plan, it's yours. Those kids have been running themselves ragged doing everything they can to help anyone that they can, never taking any type of payment for it. No matter what we offer, they always refuse. They will let us give them food and water while they are here, but that's it. They wouldn't do that if they were trying to overthrow the Council and rule over us, or were the way that you have been portraying them to us.

If you were correct in your explanation of their characters, they would come here and take advantage of our misfortune, trying to gain from it. Instead, they are coming here and helping us to overcome adversity, out of the generosity of their heart. They won't even let us barter with them. I offered them milk from my cows and eggs from my chickens. They wouldn't take it. The only response we get is they have the means to provide for their needs and they will not accept something that someone else needs more than they do."

Danny interrupts. His face is blotchy and his arms start flapping with the effort of trying to get his point across. "We have been the ones that have protected you, taken your concerns to the Council, and helped you to be able to remain living the lifestyle that you want. You want to turn your backs on us now because a group of teenagers has found a new way to manipulate you? We have seen the big picture since the beginning. We have always taken care of you. They have done many things that have hurt many people. Why would you turn against us and help them?!"

By the time he is done, Danny is yelling. A man from the fence crew steps away from the group and walks up the stairs onto the porch, he stands eye level with the Advisors. "I am not entirely certain that those kids were in control of their actions. Something tells me they are trying to make up for their past actions. I can see the guilt in their eyes. That alone tells me something is not right with this whole situation. If they had done all of those things of their own free will, why would they be trying to make up for them now?"

Noticing that nobody is going to believe anything Danny says at this point, Brian's dad tries to salvage the situation as their plan spirals out of control. "That is part of the manipulation. If they can make you believe they didn't do anything on their own, you'll feel sorry for them and help them when they ask for it."

The man sneers at him, harrumphing to himself before voicing his opinion steeped in sarcasm. "The only people I see who have benefitted in any way from this whole mess, are you four. You have the trust of all the witches. You have the power to either take their issues to the Council or ignore them. You essentially have the control over all of us. Now that there is someone else that can help us, you want us to believe they are the bad guys and you are going to protect us from them. The problem is who is going to protect us from you?"

We have heard enough. We don't want a big fight to happen. The Advisors are more powerful than the witches here and we don't want anyone to get hurt. We step out of the forest and Rayne takes great pleasure in saying, "We will."

All eyes immediately turn to us. The Advisors get smug looks on their faces, they obviously think they can bait us into doing something to discredit ourselves. We can tell that they didn't expect us to show up here, but they are quickly finding a way to use it to their advantage. The problem is, they don't realize we are not going to respond the way they want us to. And, they have completely lost the support of the witches around us. They think the others will stay out of it and that they will get the support back when they show how impulsive we can be. We know enough about them to know that is the plan.

The good thing is, they only know how we are when we are under their spell. Since they were unable to cast the spell in this lifetime, this is the first time they are dealing with the real us and not the versions of us affected by a spell that caused our own destruction. We are an unknown to them.

Claire has been quiet since she was called out on her magick, but now she has a satisfied smug smile on her face. "Of course you came back to try and make us look bad in front of those we are trying to protect from you. I'm really not surprised. You think you can just do a few good deeds and it will make up for the lifetimes worth of pain you caused? We won't let you hurt these people anymore."

She looks around at the people she is talking about expecting to see forgiving and grateful smiles. Her face falls quickly when she sees glares directed at her instead. She actually takes a step closer to her husband in response to the hostility clearly visible on the faces around her.

Chloe is still trying to pull off the carefree artist personality and tries to use it to diffuse the situation and turn it in their favor. "We know you think they are helping you. We are just trying to show you that they are only doing these good deeds so that they will look better in your eyes. They think if they can get you to not trust us to have your best interests at heart, then it will be easier for them to overthrow the Council. If we aren't in the way, it's easier for them to get to the Council. It is their master plan. If they can discredit us, and gain your trust, then you won't oppose them when they make their move against the Council."

Everybody is silent waiting for us to respond. After a few minutes, they realize we aren't going to respond to their accusations. Greg visibly scans the assembled witches, assumes they have won, and looks out at the group of people triumphantly as his chest swells slightly with pride of victory. "See? They aren't even trying to deny it! They had this planned out. It wasn't what they were trying to do, they would be doing everything in their power to make you believe them."

The wife of the man whose property we are on walks up to Greg and slaps him across the face. We stare with our jaws dropped. She looks him in the eye, her anger pouring off of her in waves. "They have come here and helped us when we needed it the most. They did not say one word about you, or the fact that you and your children have been following them around trying to undo the work that they have done, we figured it out on our own. They stayed out of the mess until it became clear you were going to try and overpower us. Then, they came out to help us with that as well.

They have never done or said anything to try and discredit you. In fact, you four are doing everything in your power to try and discredit them. They haven't sunk so low as to accuse you of doing any of the despicable things you actually have. Then, you have the nerve to stand on my porch, spout your lies about them, and disrespect all of us and our intelligence by saying that we are too stupid to figure out what they are doing?!? They don't need to discredit you. You are doing a pretty damn good job of it yourself. Now, get off my property and don't come back. You are not welcome here."

Danny opens his mouth to say something, but closes it quickly when he sees everyone around him has become hostile towards him. Rayne can't help herself, she has to say something. "I would listen to her. It looks like you are no longer Santa Claus."

We smile at her boldness, but the group of witches is viewing the Advisors like they are ready to tear them apart if they don't get moving. The Advisors are smart enough to figure out their plan has backfired. They leave quickly, but not before stopping in front of us. Danny speaks so low that only we can hear, "Just because you have a few lowly witches to support you doesn't mean anything has changed. You are still going to be the bad guys. Most of the witches will follow us and our lead. Your few weak supporters will not help you. We will win and we will have the power."

CHAPTER 23

By the time we get home, we are exhausted. It has been a long couple of weeks. We have traveled throughout the area helping where we could. It doesn't seem to make a difference. We are still overwhelmed with requests. As we look at the mail, emails, and listen to the voicemails, it becomes apparent we are not going to be able to help everyone.

We are discouraged and the adults try to comfort us. Rachael says, "If it helps, I think it is safe to say the redemption you have been trying for has been reached. It seems news has travelled about you helping and being followed. I'm sure it won't be long before everyone hears about what has happened today. The Advisors won't realize the damage that was done. They are overly confident. They won't pay attention to the other witches. They will just go on as if nothing has changed. They feel like the other witches are beneath them.

They've never gone around and helped like you guys have been doing. The other witches are seeing that. They are realizing that the Advisors treat them like subjects, and see how you treat them as equals. The Advisors always required a payment when asked to help. Most of the time, the person asking for help couldn't afford the payment, so the Advisors never had to actually help or do any work."

I let out a frustrated breath. "I know, but the problem is we have helped everyone close to us. All the requests that are left are too far for us to travel to. We can't get that far away from the Origin. If there is a threat to the Origin we have to be able to get back quickly to protect it. We can't have everyone coming here either, because that is too much exposure for the Origin. We can't have anyone figuring out what gives us our power boost. I don't know how to help those not in this area."

Ethan smiles. "I do. We set up a website. We let everyone know we are unable to travel all over the world. We can set up the website where they can put their requests in. We can then review the request, find the best solution, and give detailed instructions on how to fix the problem. We can tell them how many witches are going to be needed, and what kind of magick will be used. We can also have something on there for people to offer their services in their type of magick if it is needed for a problem.

Then, only witches that are willing to help are contacted, and the ones that don't want to be bothered won't be. We can let everyone know that there is nothing wrong with not putting your contact information in there. Everyone will understand that some people are too busy and aren't able to help. We will word it so it doesn't sound like they don't want to help, just that they can't."

Penelope is concerned. "I see the potential for a big problem with that. There are going to be some witches that are only going to put their information on there to make money on this. They are going to charge a hefty fee. Some may even sabotage others, so they are the only one with that kind of magick in an area that can help. Then the others will have to pay a large fee, or not get the help they need."

Ethan shakes his head. "I already thought about that. We can make them sign a contract with us, setting a maximum fee they can charge. If there is no one else in an area that has the same ability that is willing to help, then they must offer their services for free. There are always going to be those who try and offer their services without the website, or through this system and claim that their magick is the strongest in that area so they feel the need to charge more, but if people can get on the website and find others, then it should make it harder for the ones trying to scam."

I smile at him. "I love this idea. It also shows that we feel that everyone else is just as capable of performing these tasks as we are. We are just offering information they don't have so that they can figure out how to work through it on their own. Dad, can you set up the site for us?"

He grins. "Sure. I can have it done in a couple of days. You should respond to these requests, let them know what we are doing, and that it should be up and running in a few days. That way, they won't get overwhelmed while waiting for help. I will also put a membership requirement to be able to see the information on the site. We don't want everyone to be able to find the information and go looking for witches. We will have to figure out a way to verify identities."

Ethan is shocked. "Wow that would have been bad to just list names and addresses for the witches so anyone could find them. How would we be able to verify it?"

Rayne smirks. "Make them answer questions about us."

I let out an exasperated sigh. "Everything can't be about you."

She glares at me. "I was serious. Everyone in our world knows about us. They have been told the story as a way to control them. We ask questions that only our own people would know. We can't ask general questions, the normal people who have discovered the magick in the earth would be able to answer them. I know the groups like the Wicca are good and helpful, but they are different from us. I'm not saying we are better, just different. If we want to limit it to just us, it has to be specific questions about us."

My dad looks thoughtful. "That is a good idea. Only those that have been through a part of your history, or have been told the stories that get passed around, would know the answers. We keep the questions specific, but not about the worst of it. It will have to be on the lines of the stories, which may not always be the truth though."

I think about that and have an idea. "We could always phrase the questions to start out with, 'It has always been believed that ....' and then put the question in. That way we are not saying it is the truth, just the story that has been told."

Everyone nods in agreement. With the method settled, we start answering the requests, letting them know what we are doing. We explain about the website and the security features that will be put into place to assure that only the people of our community will be able to access the information. After a couple of days, we stop getting requests.

Everyone we talked to agreed they think this is a good idea, and we collected email addresses so we can send the link to people when the site is up. It takes my dad about a week to get it running properly, and after a few trial runs with the registration process, we finally have it ready for the others. We send out the link to the email addresses we have.

Within two days, we have so many registered witches it is unbelievable. We are excited that it is working. In the comments section, people are leaving messages about how our advice worked, and how easy it is to work with some of the witches. There are a few people who are not happy with the results, but they don't blame anyone, just ask if anyone has any other ideas.

We add a chat section. So they can work together and ask each other for advice. It is a great way to get information from someone who may have had the same problem. It opens up communication and brings people together that normally never would have interacted with each other.

After another week, the Advisors have found out about the website. We debate whether or not to approve their registration. Dad set it up to where we have to personally review each registration request and their answers to the questions, so that it will be difficult for someone who shouldn't be on the site to trick the computer into approving them. In the end, we decide we will approve them so they can see how well this system is working.

It doesn't take them long to start leaving comments. All of them are along the lines that this is our first step in overthrowing the Council. They assert that the website and registration is not Council approved, that they have advised against this, but we went ahead and did it anyway. They continue trying to convince the others we are trying to go around the Council, and that this is us trying to manipulate everyone into believing we don't need the Council anymore.

I am concerned that the Advisors will make everyone paranoid again. I have nothing to worry about. The responses to the Advisor's comments are asking why this is a bad thing. Most people can't understand why setting up a central place for people to ask questions of each other and to share experiences that can help would ever be advised against.

The more positive the comments become, the more desperate the Advisors get. They work hard trying to convince the others that we have been told not to do this, and that we are ignoring directives from the Council. The responders start ask why, if the Counsel is in hiding from us, then they would give us a directive not to create the website?

When the Advisors realize they are being confronted on their lies, they try a different approach. They infer that they had brought this kind of idea to the Council in the past to help everyone out but the Council thought the risk of exposure was too great so they would not approve it. It isn't long before people ignore the Advisors comments altogether.

When the Advisors see that nobody is paying attention to them anymore, they try to hack into the site. We aren't sure what they are trying to accomplish. Our theory is that they are going to make it where everyone can see the site to expose the contact information of everyone that has registered. My dad anticipated this and has multiple levels of security in place. They are never able to even get close to succeeding.

It is obvious they are losing support from the witches. They stop posting on the comments and they delete the posts that they had previously made. I am nervous about their reaction to the loss of support. I look over at Chase when I see they have deleted all of their comments, "They left their registration so they can still see what everyone else is posting, but they took their posts off. They have to know they are losing their hold over the witches. The power they have spent all this time gathering is slipping through their fingers. That will make them desperate and more dangerous than they were before."

Chase gives me a worried look. "I think you're right. It's not normal for them to just give up. They are the type to shove their opinion down your throat until you agree with them, not back off and walk away when you don't agree."

We go to tell the others and find out their thoughts about it. Landon is the first to offer his opinion. "I think it's all in their plan. They tell everyone how we did something the Council didn't want, and when they tried to show how bad of an idea it was and weren't able to, they stepped back. It will make it look like they gave their opinion and are now leaving it up to everyone to make their own decision. They are trying to show they trust the witches to make the right choice. When in truth, they are using it to get information and see what more damage they can do, so they can come in and rescue them to look like the good guys again."

Now I am even more worried, "You think they will intentionally harm people so they can look good in front of everyone? That is horrible."

Dale looks sad. "Those are the actions of desperate people."

CHAPTER 24

We keep a close eye on the message boards and chat sessions, watching to see if there are any signs of the Advisors creating more problems. The only thing we find are the same small problems that have been on there in the past. People are asking for advice on how to keep animals from destroying their crops, how to get rid of mice that have found their way into their house, or bug infestations. Nothing major to catch our attention as something that could have been magickally engineered.

The longer we go without anything from the Advisors, the more nervous I get. When I think I can't take it anymore, I feel it. The Advisors are here. I have learned what their magick feels like, so I know instantly that it is them. I jump up from the computer where I have been looking for any signs they were creating problems, and go to find the others.

The boys are playing video games. Rayne and Penelope are both curled up in chairs reading. When I come running in, everyone instantly look up to see what is wrong. As soon as

Chase sees the look on my face he rushes to my side. "Baby, what's wrong?"

I let the fear show in my eyes. "The Advisors are here. They're in the back yard. I don't think they know I can feel them. I don't know what they're doing. They're out by the gardening shed. They haven't moved any closer to the house though, so I don't think they are here to attack us."

I can tell Landon's mind is working at lightning speed to come up with a plan. He smirks when he figures out what to do. "Ok, they don't know Annisa can feel them, so they don't know we are aware they are here. If we want to get some information about what they are planning, we need to get within earshot of them without being seen. If we go out the front door we can circle around behind the pool house and they would never see us, but we should be able to hear them."

We nod our agreement and go out the front door. Silently, we move around the house and stop behind the pool house. Landon is right, we can hear them but they have no idea we are here.

Danny is talking. My dislike for him just gets stronger. "See how easy it is to surprise them? They don't even know we are out here. They have no security measures in place, no crystals or anything. Anyone could walk right up and attack them, and they would have no idea they were in danger. They are so confident and cocky that they can win, they make stupid mistakes like this." I start to move toward the side of the pool house, ready to let him know what I think about his attitude. Chase grabs me around the waist and covers my mouth before I can let them know we are there.

Chloe is not convinced. "How do we know that? We have no way of knowing if they know we are here, or are just choosing not to do anything. They have proven to be smarter than you have anticipated. Every plan you have come up with so far, has backfired in our faces. Even Brian and Amy no longer have confidence in us since the spell that you used to make Brian leave Amy. They won't work against us, but they have taken a step back and only grudgingly do the tasks we ask of them. We told you that was a bad plan. You continued, and now our best way of getting information will no longer cooperate with us."

Greg supports his wife. "Brian has always been curious about them. You used that to get the information that you wanted. That was fine, but when you used him and separated him and Amy, you went too far. Now we have children who can barely stand to be in the same room as us, and the whole community has turned against us.

You want us to blindly follow your lead in this? You have been wrong about everything this lifetime. We were unable to cast the spell that kept them in their endless circle and strengthened our hold, and now they are undoing every bit of work that we have done over all these lifetimes. You said not doing the spell would be fine, that we could control the witches and how they saw the situation. Those four have done the opposite of everything you thought they would. I'm not sure you are the best to lead us anymore."

I expect Danny to say something in his defense, but Claire jumps in. "Danny has been leading us since the beginning of time. It was his vision and his creativity that got us to where we are today. You want to question that now, when we are so close to getting what we have worked so hard for? This is the final stage of the plan. He never said it was going to be easy. If it was easy we would have done it a long time ago, and we wouldn't have needed those brats."

Rayne opens her mouth to defend us out of instinct, but Ethan had been expecting it and puts his hand over her mouth before any sound can escape. She looks over at us and mouths, "Sorry."

Danny sighs. "I understand your frustration. I am just as frustrated as you. I want this whole thing to be over and for us to be where we belong, in the Clouds, running everything. It will just take a little longer, and more work than we originally planned. Look how long we have been out here. We haven't lowered our voices yet nobody from the house has checked. It will be easy. We come tonight, get the four kids, restrain them in the house, and we will be able to put our plan into action. Once we frame them for destroying the Council, we will be able to rise to our rightful positions. Now let's get going. We still have some work at the house to prepare it to hold them in that room."

When they are gone, we exchange worried looks and go back into the house to work out a plan for their planned attack later. When we get in the house, get everyone in the secure room, and tell the adults what we have overheard, they are very angry. Dale's face is turning red. "They think they are going to walk into our house and take our children? Are they insane? They are in for a huge surprise when they realize we will not allow anyone in our family to be hurt."

We wait for the adults to calm down before we start to discuss a plan. It takes longer than we thought. The adults are furious that the Advisors are planning on kidnapping us and framing us for a crime they are going to commit. After about an hour, Landon is extremely frustrated. "You guys really need to calm down so we can discuss our plan."

The adults look back and forth between each other embarrassed. They seem to realize they have wasted an hour of time we could have been planning. When they have found a seat again, we look to Landon to reveal what he has come up with. He groans staring at his hands in his lap. "I can't just come up with a plan on the spur of the moment every time. This one is going to take some time. We need to discuss a few things before I can even begin to come up with something."

Chase shrugs his shoulders. "Fair enough. Where do we start?"

We wait to see if anyone has any ideas. By the blank stares everyone is giving, nobody has an idea. Finally, Ethan starts the discussion. "There are a few things we know for sure. They are no longer a united front, They are starting to mistrust each other. They are also cocky and think they are better and smarter than us. We also have the advantage of surprise. They are expecting to walk in here and catch us sleeping, not waiting for them."

I nod and add to his assessment. "We might be able to play them against each other. They are going to want to split up so we can't make any noise to alert the others that something is wrong. That means they are going to try and get to us at the same time."

Landon is taking this in. "I agree. The most likely scenario will be that they will each take one of the couples with one person as a look out. My guess would be Chloe will be the look out. She seems like she has the least amount of influence. They seem to disregard her opinion more often than not. Does that sound about right Dale?"

Dale gives us a sad half smile. "I'm glad you're asking my opinion. I was afraid since I used to be with them you would suspect me as someone helping them. I'm very happy you have accepted me into this family.

To answer your question, yes that sounds about right. From what you have told us, it sounds like Chloe and Greg are starting to doubt Danny, that could be a good thing. They could be swayed away from a plan. However, they would never give up the opportunity to rule. Chloe especially, always felt like she hasn't been given the credit that she is due. The fact that they brush off her opinions makes it worse. She is there for the power, nothing more. I believe they had never planned on her being an actual part of the new Council. I don't think that was ever shared with Greg though, he loves his wife and would never sit back and let her be treated like that. Chloe can see the way it is, but Greg thinks she is paranoid. It sounds like he is finally starting to listen to her. That could work in our favor."

Chase brings up a good question. "Is it possible Greg and Chloe are planning to take one of the couples, so Danny and Claire won't be able to continue the plan without them? It They need all of us to make their plan work."

Renae gasps, her eyes widening. "I just realized they aren't interested in Rayne and Ethan. Their whole plan has always revolved around the four of you. They don't realize Rayne and Ethan have the same power as the four of you. We shouldn't formulate a plan around them coming after all of you kids, that isn't what they are doing."

Landon groans. "You're right. Thank you. I never would have thought about that. Just because we know that Rayne and Ethan are just as important as we are doesn't mean that they do. They have seen Rayne and Ethan working with us, but they don't know that they are using the same power. They probably think we are getting a power boost from them. In that case, I think they will try and separate into two groups. Since Danny and Claire can see that Greg and Chloe are starting to doubt the plan, I would guess the teams will not be husband and wife. It is smart. If something were to go wrong, it would be better not to have your first instinct be to protect your spouse, but do what you need to do to get the job done."

I look at him in horror as my stomach knots up. "Are you saying they would sacrifice each other to obtain their goal?"

My mom looks at me with sympathy. "Honey, you have to realize that not everyone is like you. Where you would put yourself in danger to help a friend, they would throw their friend under the bus to save themselves. The only people any of them feel any loyalty to is their spouse. They have already shown that they are willing to sacrifice their own children to get what they want."

Penelope interrupts. "They didn't really sacrifice their children. Brian's parents didn't know what was going to happen. Amy's parents knew Brian would be back after the spell wore off."

Mom grabs her hand and gives it a squeeze. "None of them stepped in when Brian walked away from Amy. Her parents didn't try to comfort her at all. His parents stood by and let it all unfold. They all showed they are willing to do anything. No matter how you want to look at it, the fact is, they already have."

My face falls. I am having a hard time being able to figure

out people that are so ruthless. How can anyone set their kids up like that? How did they get to the point that they are so self-centered and heartless? A thought comes to me. "From the conversation we overheard, it sounded like Greg and Chloe didn't know about it, and resented that they made Brian not trust them anymore. It sounded like that was the event that started the breakdown. Maybe they are not as cruel as the others."

Dale is lost in his own thoughts for a minute. "I think you're probably right, Annisa. I can definitely see Danny and Claire sacrificing Amy, but Greg and Chloe adore Brian. He is the reason they do what they do. They are trying to make sure nobody can ever harm him."

Penelope interrupts him. "The reason they are doing something wrong does not make a difference. I can understand wanting to protect their son, but that doesn't excuse what they are doing, or make it right."

Rose nods her head. "You're right Penelope, it doesn't. We are just letting you know their motivations so you are able to work out a way to get this situation resolved with the least amount of damage."

Penelope acknowledges what Rose is trying to tell her. "I understand that. We need to remember that they are willing to twist things around to justify their actions."

Rayne smirks. "Um, are we forgetting that we have protection spells up around the house? They are going to find it difficult to kidnap you if they can't get into the house."

I glare at her. "You, don't have to be a smart-ass all the time. You could have just mentioned that we haven't brought them up yet."

Dale stands between our chairs with his hands out, a palm facing each of us. "Alright you two, let's call a truce. I know we are stressed but this won't fix anything. To answer your question Rayne, they have many spells that are designed for this very purpose. They have taken the spells given to them and modified them. Danny is the only one who knows how to do it, but there is a way he can manipulate the air into fooling any protection spell. We don't need to waste time trying to figure it out, or how to combat it. We need to move on, knowing that he will be able to get in."

Landon has been thinking while we have been discussing all of this. "We can't rule out that Amy will be helping them. She may be angry with them for the spell that made Brian leave, but she showed that she is still willing to help them when she put the crystals in the yard. She has always been taught that we are the bad guys and has believed everything her parents have told her. She has more loyalty to them than Brian does. I'm sure Brian isn't happy about it, but he will help her if she gets in trouble. So, we have to assume that they will be close by incase they are needed.

I think if the Advisors get into trouble, they will rush in and help. Brian has a good relationship with his parents. He won't stand by and watch if they are in danger. Amy has been raised with the belief that power is the most important thing and that it is her rightful place to be at the top."

CHAPTER 25

We pretend to go to bed around the same time that we usually do. We don't want them to think we know anything if they are watching the house. As Chase and I lay in our bed with the lights off, I am so wired I couldn't have fallen asleep if I wanted to. I have so much nervous energy running through me I could run a coffee pot. Chase chuckles and whispers "If you don't stop fidgeting they will know we aren't really sleeping in here."

I respond by childishly sticking my tongue out at him. He chuckles again, but instantly goes silent when we hear a floor board creak in the hall outside of our room. I silently roll over and rest my head on Chase's chest. He tucks his head down so he will be able to have his eyes slightly open and see where in the room they are, but it will be impossible for them to be able to tell that his eyes are open.

We wait for them to get completely inside the room to see what they have planned. We have a pretty good idea, but we don't know for sure what they are going to do to get us out of the house without alerting the adults. We have cast a protection spell around us that. It is thin and snug against our bodies so they won't be able to tell when they cast a spell that it doesn't take effect. We have designed this one to absorb the spell instead of bouncing it back to the person who has cast it. It is important that they think the spell has worked.

When they make it all the way into the room and close enough for Chase to see who it is, he opens the link into my mind. *"Looks like they find us to be the most powerful or dangerous. We have Danny and Claire in here."* He opens his mind up to everyone. *"Ok, we were wrong. Danny and Claire are working together. They must feel that Annisa and I are the biggest threat because they are in here. Landon and Penelope, you need to move on to plan B and try to maneuver your way out of it with Greg and Chloe. Remember to use their parental guilt."*

I am still not comfortable with this part of the plan, but since I had voiced my opinion already, I keep my thoughts to myself. They heard me out and listened to my concerns, but then explained why they thought this was the best way to proceed. It isn't that I disagreed that it is the best plan, it is that I don't like what has to be done. Since there is no way around it, I keep my objections to myself and remind myself that I need to focus on what is going on in my room and let Landon and Penelope focus on what is going on in their room.

I am surprised to hear Danny and Claire having a quiet argument at the end of our bed. I am amazed that they hadn't worked this out before they came into the house. I start listening to them to see if there is something that we could use against them. Claire is talking when I focus in on their argument. "All I am saying is that your impulsive spell on the kids is what caused Greg and Chloe to not trust us. Now that they are not fully on board, I think it would have been better to split them up. They are not going to go through with their end, and we will end up with these two and the other two will be free to find them.

I know, you thought Amy would understand and not

hold it against us, but the whole thing blew up in your face. Now Amy only helps because she thinks you will put her as the third member of the new Council with us, and I know where she got that idea. I can't believe you told her that. When she tells Brian, he is going to tell his parents, and we are going to have a huge mess on our hands."

I can hear the frustration Danny is feeling toward his wife in his voice. "Claire now is not the time to discuss this. I know you don't agree with all of my decisions in this matter, but you have to admit that Greg and Chloe would not be able to handle being on the Council. Amy is the best choice for our third member. I didn't just tell her that to get her to help us, I told her because it is the truth. She won't tell Brian because she wants to protect him. She is afraid if he tells his parents that they will do something to jeopardize the whole plan."

I am having a hard time staying still and pretending to be asleep. I voice my frustration in Chase's mind. *"This is killing me. Why couldn't they have had their argument before they came in the house? I don't know how much longer I can pretend to be sleeping while they argue like a couple of teenagers."*

Chase is having the same problem. *"I know, I want to say something too, but we have to be patient. We have to give Landon and Penelope time to get to Greg and Chloe."*

They have finally decided to finish their argument later and focus their attention on us. They say a spell together. When they are done, they start to walk over to us. Halfway across the room, they are stopped. They look down at the floor in confusion, not understanding why they are unable to move their feet. When they try to ask each other what is going on, they find they cannot make a sound either. The only movement they are allowed, is to move their neck so they can look around, breathe, and blink.

Finally able to stop pretending to be asleep, Chase and I stand up, grinning widely at them. Claire has a look of panic on her face, but Danny has a look of pure rage. I am really glad we rendered them speechless. I'm absolutely certain I don't want to hear what he wants to say at the moment. As we saunter over to them, Claire watches us, clearly afraid of what we have planned. Danny glares at us, as if he is trying to kill us with just a look.

By the time that we get to them, our door opens and Rayne, Ethan, Landon, and Penelope walk in. Landon is pulling Greg and Chloe behind him. They have been suspended in the same way Danny and Claire have been. Landon is using air to move them so he doesn't have to literally drag them. He places them next to Danny and Claire. Greg and Chloe have resigned looks on their faces. It seems they have accepted that none of their plans are going to succeed, and that all of their work has been for nothing. We decided that we would give them some information once we suspended them, since they would have no choice but to listen, and will not be able to interrupt.

Rayne has a satisfied smirk on her face. "I can't believe you thought we were really so stupid. Like we wouldn't have some kind of detection system to know when you were close? It was easy to sneak around the house and listen as you stood in our yard, openly confident that you are so much better than anyone else. Your arrogance is what caused all of this trouble from the beginning."

I interrupt. "We are going to give you an option you never gave us. You had us created with the sole purpose of using us as tools and getting rid of us. Despite that, we are still going to give you a choice. We are not as heartless as we think you are. The decision you make will determine if we are right about you or not."

Rayne cuts me off. "Just so you know, this was not a unanimous decision. I voted to destroy you and be done with it. I was outvoted."

I raise my brow in question and she gestures for me to continue. "She's telling you the truth. We discussed this, for a while it was likely we would just destroy the four of you. Fortunately for you, we have a conscience. We don't believe you will all make the same decision, and are pretty sure that there is so much double crossing involved in your circle, nobody can trust anyone else. After the argument you two had at the end of our bed, you confirmed our suspicions. You really should have your arguments behind closed doors so you don't give away your plans."

Greg and Chloe are glaring at Danny and Claire. Danny and Claire are glaring at me. Chase laughs and looks over at Penelope. "Just to catch you up, the two in here were planning on outing the two in your room, and making their daughter the third member in their new Council. Amy hasn't said anything to Brian because she thinks she is protecting him, afraid that if Brian said anything to his parents they would try to interfere, and Brian would get hurt in the crossfire."

Greg starts shaking as he struggles against his confines trying to get to Danny. Chloe has tears running down her face as the betrayal sinks in. Claire is wide eyed and staring. She looks lost. Danny has fire in his eyes but refuses to acknowledge anything that is happening as he stares at us.

Penelope looks over at them and then back at me. "Huh, guess it was a good thing that we knew about Amy and Brian waiting outside for a sign. I wonder how long they will stay out there and wait?"

I raise my brow in response to the shocked expressions that we know about that. I turn back to Penelope. "My guess is they are already gone. Since they didn't come in to check on their parents, I bet they thought they had been left behind."

Chase pulls a small stone out of his pocket, looks at it and puts it back. I shared when I felt Brian and Amy leave, so this is just for show to make them think that we have somehow spelled the stone to let us know when another witch was present. I realize they must use that trick themselves, answering my question about how they immediately thought we should know they were outside earlier. Chase continues our ploy, pulling me out of my thoughts. "Yep, they left. That must suck. Their own children left them on their own."

I glance over at the adults. Greg and Chloe are still glaring at Danny and Claire. Claire looks even more terrified. Looking over at Danny, I understand her fear. He is so angry that his face is red and his veins are pulsing on his throat with the strain of him trying to break free from our spell.

I turn to Claire. "Your husband is losing it. Your only friends have learned you have been planning to betray them and you've been using them. Seems you are in quite the precarious position."

Rayne can't let us have all the fun. She joins in as well. "You also have to understand the position of Greg and Chloe. They have been going along with the plans of these two for so long, they are now not welcomed by anyone now. They can't go back to their group, they are being used, and will be discarded. And, they can't find a group with other witches because of what they have done to harm others. They even stood by and watched as a spell was cast on their own son to take away his happiness. They didn't say anything, allowing their son believe that he was losing his soul mate."

Ethan decides that he wants in on this too and cuts her off. "But they do have each other. I guess that's something."

Landon adds, "Then you have the one who has been pulling all the strings. Even when everything was falling apart, and his plans were blowing up in his face, he couldn't let go of any control to let the others help and look where he is now. He has his best friends he was planning on sacrificing, his wife who is desperately trying to figure out a way that she can get out of this, whether it is with her husband or not, and his daughter who walked away and left him to deal with the fall out of his failed plans on his own. Well done. I'm glad you're not my leader."

We can see Claire has accepted that they have lost. She stands watching, but no longer trying to free herself. Greg and Chloe are looking at each other with shame on their faces, but Danny is still glaring at us and struggling with our spell. He refuses to admit defeat. Chase chuckles. "I don't think I would want to be in any of your shoes right now."

I try to look apologetic. "I'm sorry. I almost forgot we told you that we were going to give you two options. We really should stop trying to help them and give them the options so they can choose."

Penelope looks over at them. "We are going to tell you what your options are, then we are going to release you just enough for you to tell us what your decision is. If you start to say a spell, or start to rant, we will immediately take that small freedom away."

I make eye contact with each of them to make sure they understand, and are paying attention to, what I am about to say. "Your first option is to walk away. We will allow you to walk away as long as you give up your positions as Advisors, and live a normal life. If you try to gain power again we will find you, and we will take this option back.

Your second option, is to walk out of this house with no memory of who you are or what you want. We will erase all of your memories, and you will start over. You will not remember that you have magick, you will not remember who each of you are, you will not remember that you once had power, or that you conspired to get more than you were meant to have. That's it Option one or two?"

We start with Greg and Chloe. We are pretty sure what they will decide, but we are giving them each the option of choosing for themselves. When we release Greg and Chloe, they immediately turn to each other and began discussing their options.

Chloe is first to voice her opinion. "I don't care about the rest anymore. If we can walk away and show Brian he means more to us than power. We can explain to him how we were trying to make sure he was safe, and we can work on repairing our relationship with him."

Greg listens to her and then glares at Danny and Claire. "We want nothing more to do with you. No matter what you decide, when we leave this room we want to never see, or hear from you again. If your daughter will still have anything to do with you is up to her, but we intend to tell Brian everything so he will know what kind of people you are. I hope he has a stronger hold on Amy than you do. I believe she will give it all up for him." He turns and makes eye contact with me speaking for both of them. "We will walk away and you will never have another problem from us."

Danny refuses to look at them. He continues to struggle against our spell as if they are not there. Claire loses all color. She is finally realizing she could lose more than she was willing to if her daughter walks away from them too. She looks at us with panic, before turning raging eyes on her husband.

I look to the others in my group. Each nods their agreement. We release Greg and Chloe. Without another glance at the two people they have been closest to for all of their lifetimes, they turn, leave the room, and walk out of the house into the night.

When I look back, Claire has a very sad look in her eyes. I wonder if she will mourn the loss of them?. Danny on the other hand, is looking to where they walked out of the room with contempt. He obviously feels they are weak for choosing this option.

I look around at the others nervously. I see the worry in their eyes return glances. This is not going to go as smoothly. We check our spell to make sure we only give enough to let them speak. Claire looks at Danny with tears streaming down her face. "I know you want to fight and don't want to give in, but please think of Amy and me. If you fight, you won't even know who we are."

He sneers at her angrily. "You honestly believe these kids are more powerful than we are and can do what they are threatening?"

She continues to cry. "Please look at this without your bruised ego, they have stopped us at every turn. We haven't managed to put a bruise on them. We can't win this, please walk away with me! I refuse to forget our daughter. I will walk away to help her, and leave you on your own, if that is what you decide."

He looks shocked that she would leave him. He finally gets a resigned look on his face. "We will walk away." He won't give us anything more than that.

We are all stunned he gave in. Penelope has a weird look on her face but she nods her head. We release them and they too walk out of the house.

When they are gone, Penelope frowns. "This is not over. He said they would walk away, but there was deception."

Rayne nods. "There was also intent for future harm. He said what he needed to so he could get out and find a different way."

I sigh. "I thought it was too good to be true. I could tell he wasn't lying, but I wondered if it was because he was saying they would walk away tonight. He never meant they would walk away for good."

Chase yawns. "Well, that is a problem to deal with tomorrow. I don't think his ego will let him wait too long to come back and finish what he started. He won't be able to live with the fact that we got the best of them again. Let's get some sleep. Tomorrow we can deal with what comes next."

CHAPTER 26

At breakfast after we finish explaining what happened the night before, Dale and Rose exchange a look. I groan. "What? I know that look. Something is going on we don't know about."

Dale cautiously shares what they think. "Danny never would have just given up. He had another plan already brewing. He knew retreating for now was the best, but he has no intention of walking away for good. He started all of this. He may have let Claire think he was doing it for her and Amy, but that was so he would have time to convince her not to give up. He still thinks he is stronger and smarter than you. He has shown he is willing to sacrifice everything to get what he wants, he has no intention of walking away."

Rose adds "Claire knows how her husband is. She gave him a way out by wording it so he would have a bigger bruise to his ego not agreeing to it. If he fought, it would show his own selfish reasons by sacrificing his family. I think she has every intention of walking away, and she used the ploy to get him to agree, to give her time to convince him he needed to completely walk away from this whole mess too. I don't believe she will be successful. It will make Danny more dangerous. Once he realizes she will truly take Amy and walk away from him, it will make him more determined to see it through. He will only see that you have taken everything away from him, and believe if he succeeds, he will be able to get them back."

We have already figured out that is probably his thinking. It is discouraging to have it confirmed. The doorbell rings, drawing our attention suspiciously towards it. I get up and answer the door. I am surprised to see both Brian and Amy standing there. Brian asks if they can come in. I gesture for them to follow me, leading them to the dining room where we have been eating and talking. My mom can never take out her frustrations on a kid. She immediately asks, "We were just eating some breakfast, are you hungry? There is plenty."

Brian answers. "No, but thank you. We are just here to say thank you." He looks at Amy, frowning at her scowl. He continues. "Amy may not look like she is grateful, but that is because her dad is still pretty angry about last night. My parents told us everything. I wanted to thank you for giving them the option of walking away with no harm. They are not bad people. They will keep their word. Claire also came to our house to try to mend the relationship between her and my parents. I think that will take a lot of work. Danny showed up too, immediately hatching a plan to get back at you. Amy is torn because her mom told her dad she would have nothing to do with it, and now she has to choose between her parents."

Rayne is suspicious. "Why are you telling us this? More importantly, how can we know if what you are telling us is the complete story? You have shown up here twice before with the intention of getting information to take back. Now you want us to think you are here with the intention of thanking us and giving us information, why should we believe you?"

Amy obviously doesn't like the way Rayne speaks to Brian and immediately begins to defend him. "Like you're any better? You tried to tear them apart and destroy them," pointing to our group, "now you're in their inner circle. Do you really think you are the only one who can change their mind? My family is being torn apart by what you did last night. You will have to forgive me for not thanking you for that. My parents have never been on opposite sides of anything. Now, they are on opposite sides of the most important decision of their existence."

Brian sighs. "She is still pretty upset about the way this has turned out. She was promised one of the most powerful positions, and a way to protect me and our families from harm. That has been taken away from her along with her family. I think it is understandable that she is not happy about this new turn her life has taken."

I look over at Penelope and she shakes her head. "Ok, I can see that. You will have to understand though, it will take a lot more than this to make us trust you."

He nods his head. He and Amy leave quietly.

When they are gone I raise a brow at Landon. "Was there a plan behind them coming here?"

He shakes his head. "No, they came here for the reasons he said."

Penelope agrees. "There was no deception."

Rayne looks a little disappointed. "They had no intention of doing us any harm either. They came with no other agenda except to thank us."

I giggle. "Leave it to you to be disappointed that they came to apologize and nothing more."

Chase chuckles. "She wanted to be able to take some of her frustrations out on them, hoping for some kind of validation. Now she has no reason to do anything to them."

Rayne purses her lips and narrows her eyes at him. Ethan walks over to her. "Don't worry, we will be able to do something soon. Danny won't wait long. His ego won't let him."

That brings us back to reality and stops our teasing of Rayne. Rachael is worried. "He will be desperate now. He will be even more ruthless because it is not just about power for him anymore. He wants to get his family back. As twisted as his mind is, and as power hungry as he is, he will still want his family back."

Renae explains. "Claire will continue to try and convince him to back off. She will not leave him yet. She will have to prove to herself that he is not able to change before she will be able to leave. She will not help him in his plans because she is not willing to sacrifice Amy, but she will try and make him see reason."

Landon replies. "He will be on his own. He needs to win, and have his wife and daughter sit on the Council with him. He believes he can still get his goal, and that this as a minor setback he will be able to overcome."

I can't help but add "So, all we know is he will be working alone, he will do something soon, and he feels like he is in the right. We have no idea what he will do, but he will be desperate, so it will be something major. How do we prepare for it?"

My dad looks at me with sympathy. "Honey, I don't think you can prepare for it. There is no way for anyone to know what he will resort to. All you can do is keep an eye out for when he makes his move. He is desperate and grasping at straws to keep everything he has worked so hard for from slipping through his fingers."

Lydia thinks it would be a good idea for us to drive around town. "The first thing we need to do is make sure he isn't trying to distract you by harming innocent people. He knows you won't let people suffer needlessly, so we need to make sure everyone in town is alright. We don't want him to do something that will draw attention to us. We don't have the option of moving somewhere else if people get too close to discovering us, so one of our top priorities has to be the town and the people in it."

We agree this is a good idea and split up into two groups. The adults take one car and we pile into mine. As we are driving, something feels off but I can't put my finger on it.

Landon is the first one to figure it out. "It's the middle of the day, only a few kids are at the diner, and they are just sitting talking quietly. There aren't very many adults walking around either and too many shops are closed. It is like the whole town is scared. I wonder why everyone is hiding out."

That's when I can identify it. "I couldn't figure out exactly what it was, but I can sense something is off, there is a feel of danger. It is so strong that even the normal people can feel it. I don't think it is Danny though, I think the Origin is doing it, trying to warn people to stay indoors. I think it means something is going to happen today."

Ethan agrees. "I feel the same thing. The people that are out and about are trying not to be noticed. I think they are going to be heading back inside soon. The Origin must know something is about to happen and wants to help by keeping the people in the town out of danger."

The adults arrive a few minutes after we get back to the house. Derek explains the puzzled looks on their faces. "I just don't get it. Nobody is out. The few that were, looked like they were hurrying to wherever it was they were trying to go. I don't know what Danny could have done to cause this."

Landon sighs. "He didn't do anything. It's the Origin. We can feel it in the air, and if you think about it, so can you. There is a feeling of danger. The Origin is trying to protect people by making them feel like it is dangerous to be outside right now. We think the Origin knows something is going to happen today, and it wants to help."

My dad concurs. "That makes sense. At least that is one worry marked off for now. If the Origin is keeping everyone inside, it will be easier for them to remain unharmed."

I am not as relieved by this. "I agree it's a good thing the Origin is helping by keeping the people out of the way, but the fact that it needs to is worrying me even more than before. If the Origin feels the people in town are in that much danger, Danny must be planning something really big."

Everyone stares at me with shock. My mom recovers first. "You're right. The Origin only steps in to help when it is absolutely necessary. If it feels that you need to protect the people in town, Danny *is* planning something in town. We need to keep our focus there. He will try to lure people out before he does whatever it is he's planning. In town it will be something public. He will want as many witnesses that he can get. Not only will he risk exposure, but it will be harder to get to him."

Chase groans. "With a town this small, it won't take much to lure people out. Not much happens here. If he causes a big commotion, everyone will want to come out and see what is going on."

CHAPTER 27

When we get back into town, we realize we have no idea when or what Danny is going to do. The adults go shopping, acting like they are running errands so they don't raise suspicions. We go to the diner. Normally, the diner would be packed with high school kids at this time of day. There are only a handful of people here. We sit at a table in the middle of the few little groups present. From where we are sitting, we can hear the conversations of most.

We are surprised. It seems like they can feel that they should have stayed home, but at the same time they are compelled to be out. Since they are feeling both, they did the one thing that helped them accomplish both. They sit quietly inside the diner so they are still in the center of town, but they are also inside and trying not to bring attention to themselves.

We wait to see what happens when more kids stream in. Before long, the whole diner is full like it normally would be, but there is a subdued atmosphere instead of a playful one.

Some of the kids are bouncing from table to table to talk to others, but most of them find a table and sit talking quietly. With so many people here, we are having a hard time listening to the conversations around us. From what we can catch it sounds like the feeling to stay home is not as strong as the feeling to come to the diner. Hearing that the suggestion is to come to the diner, not the center of town, we are sure we are where we need to be. I whisper "This wait is killing me. I wish he would do whatever it is he is planning. I just hope that we are able to keep everyone safe and not expose our magick."

Landon has been lost in thought for a while, but now he is ready to share with us what he is thinking about. "I think the waiting is part of it. He wants to show us that he is in control. He is making us sit here and wait to see what he does, instead of trying to find him and stop him before he can do it. It really is a good plan because we can't leave all these people, but it means we are not able to search for him."

A few hours later our parents join us to get something to eat. My mom looks around and says quietly, "It's weird that all these kids are sitting in the diner all day on such a nice day. Normally, they would be down on the beach enjoying the sun and water."

We look around to make sure that nobody is paying attention to us, quietly telling them about the conversations we have heard. We all look to Dale for any ideas about what is going on. He sighs. "Honestly, I don't know what he is up to this time. Like we said earlier, he is desperate. He will probably do things now he normally wouldn't."

We accept we will have to react to what he does rather than have a plan to stop him. We order our food and eat in silence. After we finish the adults go back to the house. We are going to stay and wait for Danny to show his hand. About another hour, we start to feel a shaking in the floor. When we see the floor is starting to sink into the ground, and everyone around us starts screaming, we know Danny has finally made his appearance. We get the panicked teenagers out of the diner and into the street before anyone is hurt. We watch helplessly as a giant sink hole swallows half of the diner. We can't see Danny anywhere. Granted, many sinkholes had been popping up lately, but I am now suspecting they are not the natural disaster everyone thinks they are.

It takes us a while to calm down our classmates, trying to convince them they need to go home. I can tell that they still feel compelled to stay. I look over at Chase. "They still feel the need to stay here, he's not done yet!"

Just as I finish saying this, we hear screams coming from a building across the street. We rush to see what is going on, finding the storage room engulfed in flames. We get everyone out of the store, but they join the teenagers on the street.

Still unable to convince people to leave the area, we start looking around for what he has planned next. Screams come from the coffee shop a few doors down. We run towards it. The building is flooding from a burst pipe. Water is rushing in and people are trapped on both sides of the store. We have to find a way to get them out without using our magick. Finally, we decide the only way to do it is to convince them they have to brave the water. The pressure is not enough to force them to the ground, but it will be hard.

After some coaxing, they start to get closer to the forceful flow. After the first person is able to make it, by holding his breath and pushing his way through, the others realized they can do it as well. The ambulance, fire truck and police are now in the area, doing their best to try to keep people from panicking, and persuading them to leave. They aren't having any better success with this than we did.

When one of the old buildings starts to crack, and pieces start to fall off, landing close to the crowd, the compulsion to stay is finally broken and they scatter. We stand and watch helplessly as the beautiful old building crumples into dust. We still can't see Danny anywhere. He has himself hidden really well.

We help as much as we are able. The fire department finally gets the fire out. When everything is under control, the police officers approach us. "You were at the scene of each of these events. From what we can tell, the sink hole caused the other events, but we wanted to see if there was anything you noticed that could have contributed to what happened."

I look at him shocked, "How could a sink hole cause all of this?"

He looks at me like I should already know the answer. "When the sink hole opened up it made the ground around it unstable. The fire was caused when wires were severed due to the shift in the ground, the burst pipe was caused by the building tilting, and so was the collapse of the other building."

We explain we went to each location after we heard the screams and helped in any way that we could. We didn't see else. He is satisfied with our answers and said that we should head home.

We go back to the house. We explain what happened to our parents when we walk in. They are as shocked as we are by the amount of damage that was done.

I share what the police officer told us about the cause of the damage. Derek laughs. "Normal people will always find a way to explain what is going on around them. They will never contribute anything to magick. At least Danny didn't expose that. He is playing with you. He is showing you he has the power, he can do whatever he wants, destroying the places you love, that he is smarter and more powerful than you are. He decided to prove a point before he comes at you directly. Some of it is so he can boost his bruised ego. Some of it is to show off so his wife and daughter will realize their mistake and come back."

I sigh. "The only reason he was able to win today was because we couldn't use magick. We couldn't go looking for him and protect the people in town at the same time."

Dale nods. "That was his plan. It is how he is showing you he is smarter than you, by creating a situation where you had no good options, making you run back and forth while he was in no real danger."

I am greatly discouraged until Rose explains. "He won't do anything else in town. He can't risk being exposed or he wouldn't have a community to rule over. I think he will start to do things directly to us from now on."

Rayne raises a brow. "That's comforting. He won't play in public anymore, but that just means he will step up his game playing in private. You are basically saying today was nothing, and it is going to get worse before he finally decides to make his move."

Renae looks at her daughter, "Yes, that is basically what we expect. We have to be vigilant. He won't come directly against you to start. He will likely attempt to do something to the people you care about most. That means we, your parents, will be on the top of his list."

Rayne opens her mouth to respond with the anger that is clear on her face. Ethan grabs her hand and starts talking before she can. "Babe, we can handle anything he throws our way. We were able to keep anyone from getting seriously hurt today without the use of our magick, anything he does here we will be able to use our magick to defend against. More importantly, he will not be going after helpless people this time. Our parents have magick they can use to protect themselves as well."

She seems to calm down but she is not happy. She proves it with her next comment. "If he hurts anyone in my family, he is not going to like the way I respond."

There is no doubt in any of our minds that she means every word.

CHAPTER 28

We don't have to wait long for Renae to be proven right. We instantly know something is wrong. Our parents, who are always up before we are, are not downstairs when go to breakfast. We run upstairs to our parents' bedrooms. We are stunned by what we find. They are still in bed, and they are extremely angry, unable to move or speak. Danny did to them what we had done to him.

We free them and head downstairs. We feel guilty for giving Danny the idea. My mom picks up on our guilt. "We aren't mad about what he did. Just that he was able to take us by surprise. We should have known he would be cowardly enough to come after us while we were sleeping. He only did it to show that he could."

I look around. "I am just trying to figure out how he got in and out of here without me knowing about it. I know the feel of his magick. My radar goes off extra strong when he is around. He may know how to get around protection spells, but my radar is different."

Dale still looks really pissed. "It's because the bastard wasn't actually here. As long as he could see the house, he could cast the spell. We have used it to render a suspect helpless before they knew we were there so they couldn't run or cast a spell against us."

Rose is just as pissed as Dale. "I taught him that spell. For him to use it against us is the biggest insult."

My dad has been watching as the conversation unfolded. "It seems he got what he wanted. He wanted us to be so mad about this, that we would be distracted from the fact that he is just getting started. He is trying to throw us off balance. He knew how Dale and Rose would respond to him using that spell. He was hoping to keep us occupied with that while he put his next plan into action."

I throw shield up around us when I feel him across the street casting a spell to make us see each other as enemies instead of a family. As soon as the others feel the shield go up, everyone looks to me for an explanation. They know I sense something, but I had put the shield up so quickly they hadn't been able to sense the spell first. I explain why I reacted the way I did. "He is across the street. He cast a spell to make us see each other as enemies instead of family. I think his intention is to try to take our family away. He wants us to know what it feels like."

Chase smiles. "That is a good thing." When we gasp in shock and whip our heads around at him like he has gone insane he continues. "I didn't mean losing our family was a good thing. I meant him wanting to make us feel the pain of that kind of loss is a good thing. It means he will be focused on that goal before he tries to go after his main goal. We can keep him distracted with this until we can figure out what he plans to do."

Chase is right. "So, what do we do to keep him distracted with this?"

Rayne gets a satisfied smile on her face. "I have a few ideas. If he wants to play games, we should play games. He doesn't know we blocked his spell. It works so much better now that we have our shield absorb spells instead of bouncing them back. Whoever casts against us has no way of knowing if it actually works. We need to make him think it is working, stage a couple of loud arguments that he will be able to hear from outside."

I think about it for a minute. "From the feel of the spell, I think he was targeting couples not parent to child. He wants to break up the couples because that is what hurt him the most. Next he will go after the parents and children. That is a close second to losing his wife."

Chase grins at me. "Alright baby, are you ready to put on a show?"

I look at him warily. "I'm not sure if I can do this. We are going to have to say some very hurtful things to each other for him to believe his spell worked."

He looks at me with sympathy. "Just remember that everything that I say is the complete opposite of how I really feel. Since he can only hear us and not see us you will be able to look in my eyes the whole time and see how much I love you. I promise everything I say will be the exact opposite so you know what I am really saying."

I sigh and hang my head. I know I have no choice in this but I really don't like it. We move into the living room in order for him to hear us.

When we get there, Chase spins and looks at me with all the love he feels for me. "I can't believe I actually thought it was a good idea to marry you. What was I thinking? You are the most selfish and uncaring person I have ever met."

I can feel the sting and the hurt of his words causing tears to form in my eyes but I don't let that show in my voice. "I only agreed to marry you because I had been led to believe I don't have any other choice. I never loved you, I was following what I was told was supposed to be my destiny. I am so glad to find out now that you are plotting against me so I don't have to go through with it."

I have tears streaming down my face as I yell the words that are the opposite of how I really feel about Chase. He can't help the tears that are streaming down his face either. It is getting harder to continue to yell at each other and not let the sorrow we feel seep into our voices.

Since the spell was cast on all of us it makes it easier to get a little break and let another couple take over. Landon turns and looks at Penelope. She nods. She is ready to play her part. Landon looks away from her, unable to handle looking at her when he starts. "I am so glad it's not only me. I was trying to figure out a way out of my relationship with you. I was going to find a way to break up with you, but now that I know you are just using me for my power, it has become so much easier. I will never help you with anything again. If you want my power you are going to have to forcefully take it from me."

Penelope takes a deep breath to steady herself before she answers him. "Like I need your help, I was just fine before you came along. I had no problem with my magick until you tried to mix it with yours. Now I have nothing but problems. You have made my life miserable."

They both have tears streaming down their faces. It is killing us to have to say these things to each other. I can feel that Danny has moved from across the street and is standing to the side of the window so he can hear us better. I let the others know where he is now.

Rayne looks at Ethan and grabs his hand. This is hardest on them, having spent so many lifetimes never being able to find each other, now that they have finally found their soul mates to have to do something like this is really unbearable. Rayne closes her eyes and squeezes Ethan's hand. "I am so glad I didn't have to deal with you in every lifetime. I have been lucky enough to not have to be around someone as pathetic as you. At least I found out the truth about you before it was too late and I only had to put up with you for a couple of months."

Ethan is staring at the wall. "You are so hateful and horrible. I can't believe I ever thought I could be happy with you. You need to figure out that the world doesn't revolve around you. I am not here to be your servant. If you want someone to answer to your every beck and call, you need to find someone else. I am so done with catering to you."

Standing in the living room with silent tears running down our faces, we try to come to terms with the lies we have spouted, as well as heard. Even though we know it is lies, it still hurts to say and hear them. The adults wanted to wait until we had done our part of the show before they came in. They thought it would be easier for us if we didn't have them watching us. As soon as Ethan finishes we hear Lydia come stomping into the room. "If I have to hear one more bore me to death story about the history of anything I am going to have to shoot myself in the head. I can't take it anymore. After all of these lifetimes, I have heard about the history of everything and everybody in existence. Open your eyes and see what is around you. Get your head out of the past and realize that there is whole world right here in the present."

Derek responds, "At least I don't have to analyze and reanalyze every possible outcome of every action before I will even get out of bed. You have to think about what could possibly happen before you will even take a breath. If you would get out of your head and look around you will see that while you are over-thinking everything the world is passing you by. You are such a neurotic mess that nobody can stand to be around you anymore."

The adults are handling this so much better than we are. They are treating it as a game. They are smiling lovingly at each other as they scream. When they are done, a new stream of tears starts down my face as my parents walk in. Chase wraps me in his arms to silently comfort me as I listen to my parents yell at each other.

My mom starts. "You think you are so smart. Just because you can do computer programs doesn't mean you know everything. If you would get your head out of the computer every once in a while, you would have noticed that our marriage was over a long time ago. The only reason that I am able to pretend it is still good is because you never pay attention to anything in the real world."

My dad responds. "If I had something worth getting away from the computer for it might be a little easier. I have to hide and escape to get away from you and your constant nagging. I don't care what other houses look like, or how we would never be able to sell our house because I won't do the upgrades that you want. I don't need to live in the fanciest house you can find. I agreed to move here to get you to shut up."

Henry is next. "If you don't stop trying to shove those stupid books down my throat, I am going to burn every book in this house. Just because you feel the need to constantly live in a made up world in some book or another, doesn't mean that the rest of us want to deny reality. Books are meant for entertainment, not to consume your life."

Rachael has to stifle a laugh before she responds. "Oh and you are so much better with thinking that money is the most important thing. Money can buy objects, but it can't buy everything. If you weren't so focused on the material things, you would have figured out that the reason I am constantly lost in a book is because it is my escape from you."

Dale looks at Rose. She nods her head. He begins "Just because you are qualified to advise people on what they should do with their money, doesn't mean you can tell everyone how they should live their lives. You are so controlling that I actually look forward to my long hours so that I don't have to listen to you tell me, and everyone around me, exactly how they should be living their life, and what they are doing wrong."

Rose smiles. "At least I am not so obsessed with the inside of a person that I spend hours on end studying and cutting people up for fun. Just because you have found a legal way to cut into people to ease your morbid curiosity, doesn't mean your obsession is good for anyone."

About halfway through her tirade Danny leaves. I can feel as he gets further away. When I can no longer feel him, I look around with amazement. It is mine and Chase's turn again, but since I am not looking at him, and am instead looking at everyone else they all look back at me confused. I am still shocked by the smiles on the faces of the adults. I am not surprised at all to find that Landon and Ethan had wrapped themselves around Penelope and Rayne just as Chase had done with me.

When I am finally able to speak I tell them what is going on. "He's gone. As soon as he was satisfied that it had worked, he left. I can't believe he didn't realize we each took a turn and that no one was trying to talk over anyone else. I am even more amazed at the way that you guys handled it. How could you say those awful things about each other with smiles and loving looks on your faces?"

My mom comes over and gives me a hug. "Honey, we are so confident in our relationships that we know there is no way that anything we said could possibly be true. You are just starting out on your journeys with each other. We have had many lifetimes to get to where we are. You have never been given that opportunity. It does say a lot about each of you that you were so devastated to be saying things so hurtful to each other."

I stay in the security of my mom's arms for a few minutes. When I feel better, I walk over to sit next to Chase on the couch. As I am sitting down he grabs my hips and pulls me over so I am sitting on his lap. I look around and see that Penelope and Rayne are sitting in Landon and Ethan's laps too. Apparently the guys are not ready for us to be away from them after what had happened. I am fine with that and I snuggle in closer to Chase.

Renae is the one to break the brooding silence we are all in. "I'm sorry that you had to do that. I wish there was something I could have done to make it easier, but all I could do was watch. This is not something I should be sad not to have to do, but it reminded me of my loss. I'm glad to see you kids are taking it so well. I was afraid there was going to be some hurt feelings after what you had to say to each other.

I think Danny will let us stew over this for the rest of the day. He is going to want to drag out our misery. While this bought us time, I don't think we should play along when he comes back to do the spell to break apart the parent/child bond. Even if we know that you are confident that we don't feel that way, I am pretty sure none of us will be able to say awful things like that to you kids."

The adults nod agreement with her.

CHAPTER 29

Before we go to bed, we cast another protection shield to absorb any spells Danny might cast that night. When Chase and I get to our room, I cuddle up with him and lay my head on his chest. After a few minutes of just lying there, listening to his breathing and heartbeat I break the silence. "Do you think we will ever just have a peaceful life?"

He chuckles. "Baby, I know things are pretty crazy right now, but it won't always be like this. I think after we finish this thing with Danny things will calm down again."

I sigh. "I wish that were true. The Council will still be looking for a way to take us out of the picture. They still see us as a threat to them. They won't rest until they feel confident that we aren't able to harm them. Once we take care of Danny and they will be forced to come out of hiding and deal with us themselves. It will be even worse. They will have to be watching more than they were before."

Chase shifts so that he can look me in the eyes. "There is nothing the Council can do to harm us. I won't let that happen. You will have the life you dream of. It may not start until we take care of all of this mess, but I promise you, we will have a very happy life together."

I smile at him and pull him down so our lips can meet in a passionate kiss. While I really want to take it further than a kiss, now is not the time for that. We have to keep our focus on the area around us and not get lost in each other. As I pull back, I can see the look in Chase's eyes is disappointed but understanding. There is a promise there that we will continue this later. It takes a while for us to relax, but eventually we fall into an exhausted sleep.

I am surprised the next morning that our night's sleep had not been interrupted. We expected Danny to come back and try something else. We check the protection shield. No magick has been absorbed by it. Downstairs at breakfast, everyone else is just as confused and worried as we are that Danny had not tried anything. Penelope tries to find a reason. "Maybe he is trying to make us wait. He might think that the longer he has us fighting with each other, the easier it will be for him to do what he wants."

I shake my head. "I think he is planning his attack on the Council. He thinks he has us distracted with our fighting amongst ourselves, so he has time to plan the next stage of his game."

Landon nods in approval. "I agree. He is too impatient and impulsive to play a wait it out game. He thinks we are out of his way so he can move forward against the Council. Since we are so divided he thinks it will be easy to frame us for what he does."

My mom looks over at Dale. "The question is then, what does he plan to do to the Council?"

Dale thinks about it for a minute as we eat in silence. Finally after a few minutes he responds. "Honestly, I am not entirely sure. He had a plan before, but that included all of us. Now, he has to refigure with only him. It will be extremely difficult for him to pull off anything alone, but he is arrogant enough to think it is possible. He always thought we were just there to assist him when he wanted us to."

Rose adds "Claire was the one who would convince him that he didn't need to do everything alone. She was the one that kept him on a sane level. Now that he doesn't have her to rein him in, his ego is going to be huge. She knew how to word it so it sounded like he came up with the idea. She was really good at manipulating him into doing it the best way, instead of barging in throwing his weight and magick around."

Landon decides to share his theory with us. "It sounds like we know what he is going to do then. If he has always been impulsive and reckless, and just wanted to barge in with guns blazing, that is exactly what he is going to do this time. He will think he should have just done it his way in the beginning instead of listening to her and that the only reason everything has been blowing up in his face is because the others were holding him back."

Dale nods his head. "I think you're right Landon. We just have to figure out where the Council is hiding out and we will know where he is going to strike next. I knew where they were, but I'm sure they moved when I left the group. I'm also sure they moved again when Greg and Chloe left the group. They are smart enough to see that everything is falling apart for the Advisors. They would not have contacted Danny to let him know where they are now. I think it is safe to assume they know they can't trust him anymore, and are probably looking for new Advisors."

Renae smiles. "They won't be able to look for new Advisors and stay in hiding at the same time. They will either have to show themselves, or wait to locate someone they feel they can trust. I personally don't think they will replace the Advisors. The last time they instilled more power in someone, it backfired worse than they ever imagined. They will be hesitant to do it again after the mess that was created with these four. I'd bet that they have figured out Danny's plan to overthrow them and use the kids as scapegoats too."

Derek nods his head. "I agree. They won't trust anyone

enough to create new Advisors. I also think that will piss them off. It means they will have to spend more of their time watching us themselves instead of just having someone report on what is going on. They are all about their luxury and not having to actually do anything. They won't like that they have to lift a finger to take care of these problems. I think they are hoping that we and the Advisors just destroy each other, taking care of the whole mess for them."

Dale smiles. "I'm sure that is what they are hoping for. Good thing for us that isn't going to happen. They only have a few hiding spots. Since there are two that they can't use, it only leaves two others. It won't be hard to find them. Also, fortunately for us, they can't hide in the Clouds. They have to be here, which means we should be able to find them."

Everyone looks at him shocked by his words. We have to lift our jaws up off the table. Landon is the first one to recover his ability to speak. "They have been here this whole time? Why would they just hide here where anyone can get to them instead of staying in the Clouds where we can't go as long as we are tied to our human body?"

Dale continues to smile. "Those questions are exactly why they hide out here. The downfall for them, is they can't watch or listen in, so they have no idea what is going on. They have to rely on rumors. They are very good at not being seen. I'm sure they know you have managed to redeem yourselves with the witches, and that the Advisors are no longer useful. The problem is, Danny will be able to find them just as easily as we will."

Rose laughs. "We have a head start though. He will come back to make sure we are still distracted by his spell. He won't do that until he is ready to go against the Council. If we leave now, we will be able to find them first and can be ready when he gets there. He might be confused as to where we are, spend some time looking for us even, until he decides it doesn't matter right now and that he will be able to find us after the fact."

We get ready to head out to find the Council. We split up

into the two groups we usually do. The adults are in the car ahead of us and we are following. Chase is driving because I am nervous about meeting the Council and how they will react to us showing up. Penelope is just as nervous as I am and she asks "How do we know they won't try to kill us as soon as they see us? They already think we are a threat, so for us to find them while they are in hiding doesn't sound like the best plan."

I nod my head in agreement. Ethan tries to calm our fears. "They will see that they are outnumbered and will try and manipulate their way out of it. While they are trying, we will be able to explain why we are there. They won't do anything that could result in them being harmed, they will let us protect them from Danny and won't do anything to stand in the way of that."

We ride the rest of the way in silence. When we get close to an area where I can feel powerful witches, I send a text to my mom. To keep the Council from figuring out what we are doing, we drive by them without looking at them. When I feel them, we know where they are. We have been driving for over an hour. I am glad that we are able to find them. I am too nervous to sit in a car much longer. We pass the spot where they are and park about a block away.

When we get out Dale has some last minute advice. "They will know we are coming. I'm sure that they have spies watching and reporting to them. They will try to talk their way out of it because there are so many of us. We need to explain why we sought them out quickly. Their sense of self-preservation should make them accept our help. For the time being you are safe. They will be too worried about harm coming to them."

We nod our heads in understanding and start walking. When we get to the group of cabins, everyone looks to me to know where to go. I walk straight for the third cabin. We get to the door and pause. We look around to see if there is anyone visible. Of course, whatever spies they have are well hidden. I'm certain the Council on the other side of the door knows exactly how many people are standing out here, and who we are.

Now that we know where they are, the adults make their way to the front of the group. They are going to go in first in case the Council panics, then it will be them instead of us that are hit by any spells. We have cast a protection shield around all of us to prevent any damage or injuries, but there is always the chance they will be able to get around it.

With a last look over his shoulder to make sure we are ready, Dale nods his head and opens the door. We walk into the spacious cabin. I am stunned to see three men in suits sitting in wingback chairs, and three women talking quietly while they are making food in the small kitchen area. The men smile at us as the one in the middle starts talking. "It took you long enough. We were beginning to think you were going to let Danny find us before you showed up."

The adults let out the breath they have all been holding. We stare in disbelief.

CHAPTER 30

The women in the kitchen chuckle and go back to preparing food. The men laugh at our expressions. The one I recognize from our vision as the one that handed down our punishment, has brown hair and hazel eyes. He introduces himself. "My name is David. The strawberry blonde over there is my wife, Anne." She turns and waves. Her green eyes sparkle with amusement.

The one with hair so blonde it looks white, with pale blue eyes is next. "My name is Jon. The black haired beauty over there is my wife, Sara." Sara turns and waves. I see sympathy in her dark brown eyes.

We look to the last Council Member. He has blonde hair and green eyes. He smiles and takes his turn. "My name is Justin. The brown haired vixen over there is my wife, Lisa." She turns and waves, but she has caution in her blue eyes.

It seems David is the spokesman for the group. "There is no need to introduce yourselves, we know who you are. I'm sure you are surprised we know so much about what is going on. You really shouldn't be. What kind of Council would we be if we relied on only three people to keep us informed?"

Rayne starts to say a smart ass comment. I see Ethan squeeze her hand in warning and she swallows whatever it was that she was going to say as she frowns at him. David waits to see if any of us are going to answer his question. He shrugs his shoulders like it doesn't really matter if we answer or not. "The way we figure it, you have about an hour before Danny decides he doesn't care where you went off to and starts his search for us. We have known for quite some time about his ambitions to take over our roles. He has never had the right circumstances to accomplish this until now. Since it was your group that provided him those circumstances, it is your responsibility to fix this little problem."

My jaw drops. Nothing can keep Rayne from making her comments however. "No need to thank us for coming to save your sorry asses. We didn't have anything better to do, so we thought we would come here, get insulted, and save you. Your gratitude is overwhelming."

We groan at her comments. Really, what is she trying to do, get us killed? Fortunately, the Council finds her amusing. Justin looks at the others. "She has always made me laugh. I love her attitude. It will come in handy for her later in life I'm sure."

Again, we look at the Council in shock. Surely I heard them wrong. I am so confused I can't put a full sentence together. Landon seems to be the only one keeping his wits about him, but his comments are not any better than Rayne's. "Why should we help you? It would seem almost justified to see how you fare against Danny by yourselves. After everything you have put us through, now you expect us to just waltz in here and save you from the mess you created? Then we get to go home and wonder when it is you decide to do something else to us?"

Unlike Rayne, Landon doesn't amuse them. Jon looks at him with fury in his eyes. "You dare to come in here and threaten us? Who do you think you are? It is the responsibility of all to protect us. We are the reason you are here. We are the ones that brought each of you into this life. We are the reason any of you exist."

Rayne looks over at Ethan. "Wow, touchy subject. Remind me to steer clear of the whole 'I made you' argument. That could get annoying really fast."

This time they are not as amused at her comments. Dale can see that this is quickly becoming a situation none of us wants to be in and tries to bring the conversation back to safer topics. "We are not here to discuss how we became to be, we are here to stop a crazy man. We need to come up with the best way to deal with this so nobody gets hurt."

David waives his hand like it is no big deal. "That's easy. You just need to kill him and eliminate the threat."

We stare at him with our mouths agape in shock. It is Chase that responds this time. "We are not going to kill anybody. We will erase his memory and he won't remember that he has magick or that he was trying to obtain more power than he was meant to have."

David has a blank look on his face like he doesn't understand what Chase is talking about. "You had no problem killing Peter and his threat was just to you. There should be no reason you won't kill Danny when his threat is to us which is exponentially more important."

We thought Danny had an ego. I am wondering how we are going to be able to work with them when they think the only acceptable plan is the one they came up with. I have no intention of killing anyone else. I look over at Rayne to see how she is handling the flippant way David talks about her father's death. She is doing about as well as I expect. Her face is red with anger. Ethan is whispering something in her ear, trying to calm her down before she does something she will regret.

The women bring in a tray of sandwiches from the kitchen. There is plenty there for all of us. They take seats next to their husbands. We sit and eat in silence, trying to find a way to bring our plan up and make it the one that will be implemented. I decide to try my hand at talking some reason into the men who have no consideration for anyone but themselves. "I understand that killing Danny is not permanent. He will be cycled through and will come back. I think it would be a far worse punishment to make him forget everything. He won't even remember his name.

He has done everything to make sure he is in control. The worst thing we can do to him is take that control away. He will have to depend on others to survive. His wife and daughter will have to take care of him. He will have lost all of his power over the other witches, and won't remember he has magick, so he will have no idea how to use it."

Chase and Landon both look at me with impressed expressions. I have worded our plan in a way that it is more appealing to the Council than just killing him and being done with it. David considers my proposal. "I believe you are right. It would be a far worse punishment to take away everything he holds dear and important. We will allow this plan of yours instead of killing him. However, if he regains his memories and tries to come after us again, it will again be your responsibility to stop him."

I agree to his terms. "The spell I am planning on using to erase Danny's memory will not fade. When he dies, he will still not remember he had ever been an Advisor to the Council. I am not going to bury his memories, I am going to erase them from existence. When he is reborn in his next cycle and his memories come to him after his 16th birthday, he won't be able to retrieve the memories of his past lives. But, others he convinced to go along with him will be able to remember. They will know what happens when someone goes against the Council."

I add the last part for the drama factor. The Council seems to thrive on drama, so I tried to play into that. David smiles. "I think that is an excellent idea. It is always wise to remind the witches we can't be touched. We will always win."

I hold my hand up to stop his sure to be lengthy bragging session. He is not impressed that I interrupt him. I don't really care at the moment. "Danny is about a mile away. We should get ready."

The Council gives me a questioning look and I realize that I have just given away my ability to sense other witches. Thankfully, I am able to think fairly quickly. I grab the crystal I had put in my pocket. I hold out my hand and show them. "I placed a spell to know when he was near."

It seems to satisfy them. I let out a long slow sigh of relief. We don't have much time to figure out a plan. We have the basics and we are going to have to come up with the rest as we go along.

We move the Council and their wives into the den at the center of the cabin. It is a room we are able to close off and protect from all sides. It is the safest place for them. We place a spell around the room that won't allow anyone to enter or exit. The Council is not happy about being inside, but we need to know they aren't able to attack us from the back while we are fighting Danny.

Danny stops about a block before the cabins and walks the rest of the way. He has no way of knowing we are here, or that we know exactly where he is. The adults move to the kitchen to stay out of our way, but still be close enough to help if we need it.

When Danny gets to the house, he circles it to see if there is a way he can slip inside unnoticed. He sees the open bedroom window and goes to it just like we hoped he would. His arrogance really is going to be his downfall. If he had thought about it in the least, he would have realized that one open window was probably a trap. When he comes sneaking down the hallway we are waiting for him in the living room. We use the same approach to intimidate him that the Council had used on us.

When he rounds the corner we look up and Rayne greets him. "It's about time. We were starting to get bored waiting for you to figure out where to go."

He looks at us with a confused expression on his face. "What are you doing here? The Council wants to destroy you, and you hate each other. There is no reason that you should be here."

We laugh. Penelope looks over at me. "It really is amusing to watch someone who thinks they have it figured out, and then realize everything they thought was wrong."

Chase smirks at Danny. "It was staged. Your spell never made it into the house. It was absorbed by our protection shield. We just put on a show for you to make you think you were winning."

Landon adds "The Council may want to destroy us but saving themselves is more important to them. They will allow us to save them and will get back to their original diabolical plan later. Even though we are saving them, we aren't stupid enough to think they will back off. We'll deal with it when they decide what it is exactly that they want to do.

It seems their plans regarding us have blown up in their faces and they need more time to figure things out. See, that is where you are different. Even though their plans keep blowing up and falling apart, they stop, reassess, and find a different way. You, just keep barreling forward and expect it to fall into place for you."

I stand up. "I'm sure you are really confused as to why we are telling you this. It is simple, you won't remember any of it. I wasn't joking when I said we were going to erase your memory. You will remember your basic body functions, other than that, you will have no memory. Not your wife, your daughter, that you have magick, how to use magick, or anything else. You will no longer have control of anything."

While he looks at me with shock, and before he can react, I say the spell that will erase his memory. When it hits him his face falls into a completely blank mask. After a few minutes his face goes from blank to confused. "Where am I? Who are you and why is everyone staring at me?"

We call Claire to let her know where we are and what was happening. She sounded resigned on the phone, but assured us she would come get him. She shows up not long after the spell is cast.

She walks into the house with Amy close on her heels.

Amy glares at us then studies her dad. "Daddy, are you alright?"

He stares at her blankly. "Who are you, and why did you call me Daddy?"

Amy bursts into tears and runs out of the house into Brian's arms, who was waiting outside knowing what would happen.

Claire looks at her husband and talks to him in a calming manner as if he is a wild animal that has been backed into a corner. "Your name is Danny. I'm Claire, your wife. That was our daughter Amy. I know you don't remember any of this, but I promise, I am here to help you. Please come home and we will get through this together."

He looks at her for a minute. He walks over to her and she looks back at us. "Thank you for taking mercy on him. I promise you won't hear from us again."

He looks between her and us. "What do you mean for taking mercy on me? What happened?"

She sighs. "I'll explain when we get home. Come on, we need to get going."

They walk out of the house. We turn toward the angry faces of the Council. They are standing inside the open door, but unable to cross the threshold. Now that Claire has taken Danny and left, we feel it is safe to let them out of the den.

"Well now that everything has been cleaned up, we can finally go home." Without a word to us or even a thank you, they disappear.

We pile back into the cars and head home. Back at the house, we immediately go to the secure room. Dale begins. "That went better than I thought it would."

Renae laughs. "It only went well because we thought to lock the Council in a room and not allow any magick to enter or leave where they were. The Council had every intention of attacking while the kids were busy with Danny."

Rayne smiles. "That's why I made the suggestion to trap them in there like that. I could feel their intent for harm and it was present, not future."

Landon laughs. "I could sense the strategy and plan as soon as we walked into the cabin."

Penelope smiles "The deception was so thick in that room that I was having a hard time figuring out who was deceiving who. I think their whole existence is centered on deception."

I sigh. "I hope we at least get a little bit of a break before they send something else after us. I would really like to enjoy some of our summer break from school. I don't want to spend the whole summer fighting off whoever, or whatever comes after us next."

Chase pulls me close. "I think we will be fine for a while. They are going to want to show that this is what happens when you try to conspire against them. They aren't going to want anything to happen to us until that has been spread, and everyone has the opportunity to confirm the stories." He looks around taking in the weariness of the group. "And, the best way for them to get confirmation is to ask the ones directly involved. Now that we have redeemed ourselves with the witches, they will believe the story when we tell them it is true. It also means that since we saved the Council and protected them, it eliminates them being able to use any witches in the future to come after us."

I smiled, "That means our biggest threat has been taken care of. If the witches won't be coming after us then what could they possibly send that could be worse?"

My dad looked at me with sympathy, "Honey, you would be surprised what is out there, and how bad it can be."

My face falls in defeat at his words. He laughs. "I'm sure you will get a little time to recoup before the next threat presents itself. Don't worry about what may be coming, just enjoy your life and deal with each problem as it presents itself."

ABOUT THE AUTHOR

Miranda Shanklin resides in Central Illinois with her husband and their two children. When she is not working at her day job as a paralegal, running her children to practices or supporting them at events she is writing. She has been an avid reader most of her life and has always dreamed of writing her own books someday. Now that her children are reaching their teenage years she is finding the time to sit down and chase her dream.

Miranda can be found on her website www.mirandashanklin.com or Facebook at www.facebook.com/mirandashanklinauthor

Made in the USA
Middletown, DE
29 March 2023